GHOST OF THE NEON GOD

T.R. NAPPER

TITAN BOOKS

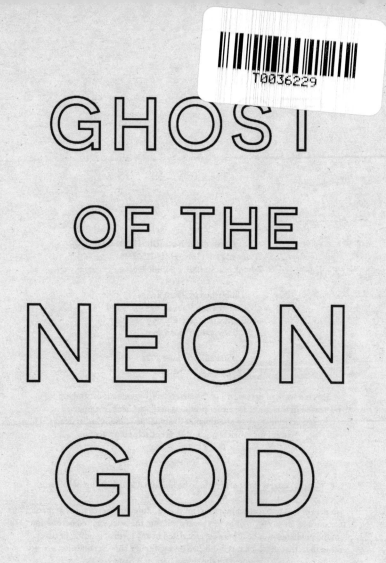

Ghost of the Neon God
Print edition ISBN: 9781803368115
E-book edition ISBN: 9781803368146

Published by Titan Books
A division of Titan Publishing Group Ltd
144 Southwark Street, London SE1 0UP
www.titanbooks.com

First edition: June 2024
10 9 8 7 6 5 4 3 2 1

This is a work of fiction. All of the characters, organizations, and events portrayed in this novel are either products of the author's imagination or are used fictitiously. Any resemblance to actual persons, living or dead (except for satirical purposes), is entirely coincidental.

A CIP catalogue record for this title is available from the British Library.

Printed and bound by CPI Group (UK) Ltd, Croydon, CR0 4YY.

"Constructed with the nuance, wit, and sniper-precise obversion to make you believe and fear his hard-boiled vision of the future."
Luke Arnold, author of *The Last Smile in Sunder City*

"A delirious turbo charged road movie narrative filled with unexpected left turns and terse, snapshotted character-work gold. T. R. Napper is fast turning into my go-to for all that's good and fresh in what cyberpunk has become"
Richard Morgan, author of *Altered Carbon*

"*Johnny Mnemonic* in the Australian Outback with some *Ghost in the Shell* ruminations on the future of artificial intelligence. A cracking good read; T. R. Napper is one of the best SF writers working today."
Richard Swan, author of *The Way of Kings*

"Relentless energy, breakneck pace, wired with countless ideas and inventions, all of them utterly convincing and harmonised into the siren song of a terrifying future. "
Jock Serong, author of *The Rules of Backyard Cricket*

"Raw, classic cyberpunk ... Napper always nails grounded characters dealing with big questions. It'll grab you from the first line and will not let go."
Timothy Hickson, author of *On Writing and World Building, I-III*

"Loved this atmospheric, fast-paced ride through a future in which society's fringe slams headlong into terrifying techno potential."
Cat Sparks, author of *Lotus Blue*

Also by T. R. Napper and available from Titan Books

36 Streets
The Escher Man

For Sarah

PART ONE

Ghosts of a Neon God

"Circumstances have forced us to become what we are – outcasts and outlaws, and, bad as we are, we are not so bad as we are supposed to be."

Ned Kelly, The O'Loghlen Letter (1879)

Cigarette dangling from his lips, Jack Nguyen jimmied the panel at the back of the glimmer bike. Col Charles stood in the shadows at the head of the alley on lookout, softly whistling an aria. The bike was a wide-bellied easy rider belonging to one of the wide-bellied, handlebar-moustached Rebels bikers playing pool in the dive bar backed by the alley.

Sweat rolled down Jack's temple as he took a long drag on his cigarette, orange point the only light visible in the dark. His cheap infra-goggles good enough to show the outlines of the shimmer-smooth control panel; that, and the crude scar cut into the back of his hand – *4007.*

The security on the bike was above average, but unimaginative. A hundred panels waited, just like this, in the labyrinthine alleys, the multi-level underground car parks, in the back lots and back streets of the city.

Jack popped it, pulled the drive card, fried the GPS node, and slipped it into his pocket. Any petty crim who wanted their spinal cord intact was smart enough to leave Rebels' glimmers alone. True. But it was also true that Col and Jack valued a full stomach over a spinal column, right at that moment. And anyway, Jack was young enough to feel eternal. Col was a nihilist, which was the same thing, more or less.

Jack pinged Col through their neural link; Col left his post, ghosted back along the alley. They walked side by side down in the darkness, quickly, through left and right turns towards the tram lines. Sweat prickling the backs of their necks, stomachs bunching into knots as they rounded each corner, waiting for a steel-toothed outlaw to take to them with a baseball bat.

Eternal, sure, but the Rebels were still the Rebels.

One turn from the tram stop, under the neon glow of an *EE-Z-CREDIT* sign, they heard the footsteps. Jack drew the double-edged blade strapped to the small of his back, Col his snub-nosed revolver.

A shadow flitted around the corner, footfalls pounding. Jack pulled back his weapon, too late, the body colliding with his. He lost balance, fell, his knife skittering on the concrete.

When he got to his knees, Col was pointing his gun at a Chinese woman while she spoke rapid-fire in Mandarin, palms open in surrender, also on her knees.

Jack's neural implant translated the words, two seconds after they left her mouth.

"[...soon. Money, I can give you money if you help me. I work for *bleeeep*. I came here to–to meet a man from *The Age*. Reveal the truth about the next-generation *bleeeep bleep*.]"

Col's face was side-lit by neon, his half ear and scarred cheekbone visible. He licked his lips, uncharacteristically lost for words, glancing back towards the street, the people bustling past in the light. No-one saw the trio ten feet in, or at least they all pretended not to.

"Who's after you?" Col asked.

She replied: "[*bleeeep bleep*.]"

Col said: "Hmm. Bleep. Sounds serious."

She looked confused. She also looked, well, beautiful. Even in the dim alley, Jack couldn't help but notice her short, shimmer-healthy black hair. The woman had the kind of skin you kept after twenty-five years of good nutrition, little sun, and no cigarettes. Slightly upturned nose, long neck, lips wet. She held her shoulders straight, regal somehow, even as she was on her knees, even as she faced off two thugs in a dark back alley on a steaming city night.

It was beauty of a kind Jack wasn't used to seeing in the flesh. Marred only a little by the fear that tightened her jaw.

Col continued: "If it's serious enough for my translator to censor it, then you have a problem no amount of lucre can fix, especially by two petty crooks." Col was now haloed by the neon glare, so Jack couldn't see his expression. But he caught the intent in his words easy enough. "We got no time for the conspiracies of the red aristocracy, or their scions. But I have time for those shoes—" he pointed at them with the nose of the revolver "—Fujian original, I'd wager – good for two ounces of weed, box of untracked bullets, couple of real meat burgers in Fitzroy."

"Shit," said Jack.

"Exactly," said Col.

Jack looked at the woman. "Give him your shoes, lady."

She looked between the two, perfect eyes wet with terror. Jack's breath caught, at those eyes. He swallowed, tried to maintain the bravado.

She said: "[You *must* help me. You must do *what is right*, and restore harmony. The fate of your country rests on this.]" She held out her hands to Jack. Knowing, somehow, he was the weak link. Slid her fingers over his hand, fearless, her other brushing his neck, behind his ear.

Jack batted her hand away. He felt a tingling sensation at her touch, surprise at her courage.

"We don't have a country," said Col, "and restoring harmony – well, that's a bit above our station. Now," he pointed the handgun at her head, "yer fucken shoes."

She did as she was ordered – jerkily, a robot in need of an oil change – and got unsteadily to her feet. She dropped the shoes, eyes already elsewhere, then stutter-stepped into a run, into the darkness.

Col raised his eyebrows at Jack, smiling, and scooped up the prize.

Jack, still on one knee, looked for his blade. His lip bled. Probably bit it when he collided with the woman. He wiped the sweat from under his eyes, fingertips shaking, just a little. "My knife," he said.

Col waved the gleaming black leather shoes at him. "I'll get you a better one. Let's get out of here."

Jack took one look back down where the woman had run. Already gone, without a trace. He sighed, and followed Col.

◇

They waited at the tram stop, watching the traffic go by. Glimmer bikes and hydrocars and autobuses, frenetic and frightened in the steaming, sizzling, Melbourne night air. Fifty years past relevance. Even fifty years ago it was the peripheral: to Asia, the oceans, the Earth. Now it may as well not have even existed.

Past midnight, shirts soaked with sweat, they hopped off the tram at the end of the line and walked on aching legs into the construction zone, an unfinished second CBD for the city.

Col's cochlear-glyph implant gleamed behind his left ear. The cool circle of steel everyone over the age of twelve had embedded. Each with its control jack and a memory pin. Theoretically removable pins, that almost never were. Recording their memories and connecting their minds to freewave, forever.

Not Jack and not Col, though. Theirs were long gone. It sucked being disconnected, but better than having a record of their illegal activities for easy viewing by the authorities. Col said their minds needed time to breathe anyway. That constant interface with the freewave made them more malleable for the megacorps, stunted their individuality.

Jack didn't know about all that. He just wanted to watch the cricket, and a few yuan gave him a PoV grandstand seat right behind the bowler's arm at the Members' End.

Through half-completed office blocks, past complete but empty restaurant strips. Through shadows cast by the future. Col whistled Vivaldi, *Winter*, pitch perfect. Light came from the pale moon, from the neon company signs on the towering yellow cranes, high above; from twenty-gallon drums, where groups of sallow-faced transients stared into the flames and made no conversation.

The young men eased themselves through a hole in a chain link fence, over the dusty ground, and through an exit they'd hacked. Forty-eight bare plascrete flights. First part of their security system; cardio wasn't big among the malnourished homeless or the street thugs. Second part was a security swipe Jack had coded to their thumbs. The third part Jack hoped they'd never have to use.

Puffing, they walked through the huge office space, bare hard floors, wiring dangling from the walls. Col paused, looked around the dark, cavernous space, doing his thing: seeing things Jack would never see. "These labyrinthine and endless rooms, doors, and stairways, they lead nowhere."

Jack pointed at the engraving next to the door. "Nah, mate, this leads to the kitchen, see?"

Col blinked, then pressed his lips together. Jack walked into the next room, smiling.

Jack flicked the lights. The room was in the centre of the structure, windowless. Surveillance drones shouldn't be able to pick up the light. If they were rigged with thermo-optics they were kind of fucked, but the only citizens who could afford the high-end stuff didn't live in these parts.

The meeting room was long, white walled, even carpeted. The kitchenette in the next room, like the lights, functioned after Jack had connected up the wiring to the glimmer glass that coated the building in solar particles. Cooling, too, when they wanted it. Best accommodation either'd had in years.

Jack dumped the drive card and goggles on the long plasteel meeting table that dominated the room. It was strewn with instant noodle packs, stripped copper, a baggie of black-market tobacco, and a flexiscreen he still hadn't managed to hack. He grabbed his comic from the table edge, went through the kitchenette – salvaged toaster, three-day old bread, gas camping stove on narrow benchtop – and into the bathrooms.

Jack ran his fingertips reverently over the dark cover of the comic. A man with a briefcase, casting blue shadows on a wall. Shadows filled with the faces of people. Faded, just the name *100 Bullets* legible on the front cover. Stolen from some wealthy bastard's Tesla Europa. A real book, comic book anyway, just sitting there on the passenger's seat.

He sat on the toilet, found his place, absorbed. When he'd finished he used the bucket to flush. Hauling water forty-eight floors a definite downside to the accommodations.

When he got back out Col was at the long table, drinking a bottle of water, eyes closed as he savoured it. Cooled, right from the unit in the kitchenette. The light picked out Col's scar, dirty purple, running straight from a point near his nose round to his missing half ear. Druggo, ice-seven trance, had come at them with a samurai sword when they were trying to score down in St Kilda.

The woman's shoes were on the table, black and shiny. Col's battered .38, cylinder popped and empty, rested alongside.

"That true about being able to get some bullets?" asked Jack.

"They're real leather. A box of bullets, GPS dot removed. Sure."

"Any left?" asked Jack, pointing with his chin.

Col reached inside his jacket, pulled out a foil-covered package. A very small one. He placed it on the table in front of him, carefully unfolded the foil. "Yeah. For tonight, anyway." Col pulled some papers from the same pocket and started rolling, spider fingers dancing, conjuring two perfect joints.

"That woman," said Jack.

"Yeah?"

"What was she going on about?"

"Trouble."

"She seemed pretty intense."

"Rich people always get intense when something doesn't go their way."

"Col."

Col looked up from his joint. "Jack. She was pretty, I get it. A damsel in distress. But she, and her problems, are out of our league. Out of our fucking galaxy, mate."

"Yeah," Jack said, a non-answer.

"We've had a long, hard day of petty crime, comrade." He held up the joints. "We need to unwind."

"Yeah," said Jack, a real answer.

◇

Two floors up to the open air. Jack hadn't figured a way to disconnect the smoke alarms in the building, so they had to pop the access panel to the roof. Easier to break into one of these places than smoke in one. They sat on the half-metre ledge, legs dangling over infinity. The neon city shimmered out to the horizon, unstable somehow, under Jack's eye.

"This," Jack held up the joint, and pointed it at the scene, "and that view. Makes this city seem like – like something else."

"Yeah?" asked Col. Interested.

"Yeah. Like it's not all real, you know?" Jack's eyes were glazed. "Like it's part illusion. Like it's…" He trailed off.

"The information isn't in the drug. It's in you."

"Yeah?"

"Yeah. Opens the doors of your perception. *Your* perception."

"Nah, mate," said Jack. "Pretty sure it's the joint."

"Your information is right, Jack. This city runs over with ghosts and neon gods."

Jack nodded, not understanding, and passed him the joint. It looked like Col wanted to make a speech; harder for him to do it supping on a J. Col inhaled, orange tip flaring against the darkness, while Jack took that small space to absorb the quiet.

"Gotta move out soon," said Col. "The government rolled over on their latest claim, so Chinese money's coming back in."

"Huh?"

"Chinese claim over North Vietnam."

"Oh. Where'd you get all this information?"

"The news, dickhead, like everyone else."

"Oh."

"Thought you'd know about that."

Jack straightened. "Why?"

Col shrugged. "Yeah. Sorry mate."

Jack looked at the yellow crane, the number *789* emblazoned in red neon on its cab, towering over a giant hole in the ground, one lot over. Fingers of ochre rebar reached out from the walls of the pit, under the construction lights. The lights had come on a week back, stayed on. "Yeah," said Jack. "The crane's been moving again. I heard Three Toes Molly lived up in one of those for a while. Wind kept her awake."

"There's no solitude, anymore," said Col, looking out over the city, swapping without explanation to the conversation he wanted.

This is what Col did, instead of uni – ruminated from the top of abandoned buildings. He should have been doing it on a campus. Smarter than most of those rich cunts. Talked just like them, too, especially when he was getting high. "There's no contemplation, no quiet choices," Col continued. "No place to be alone, even in our own heads. We are a product of the freewave. The *single most* important product. Every moment we use it we contribute to the knowledge of the mega-corps. Monetising our data freely, willingly giving them the information they need to perfect their control."

"Sure no contemplation with you talking all the fucking time."

"The freewave is central now to what we do as a species. Indispensable."

Jack inhaled.

"Ever wonder if we actually exist?" asked Col.

"Shit. Mate. Seriously. Have another toke."

Col accepted the doobie, did as asked. Then continued:

"When our decision-making is nurtured by corporate algorithm, when so many of our experiences are *their* simulations of experience, when we've outsourced our memories to be stored and filed away, by them. When our every moment is sampled, deconstructed, and rebuilt back into Trojans – advertising, architecture, news reports – that reformat our lives. How can we exist, then, when we're someone else's dream? They create these cities, Jack, and cities are huge external memory devices. But the memories are not ours, always those of others."

He waited, like Jack was meant to say something. So Jack said: "Yeah."

Col continued: "They create the spaces within which we live our lives, moulding us to fit into the places they define – public or private, park or car park. We are created and re-created by our spaces. It's a constant feedback loop. Space shapes behaviour – what you can do in it, what you can't. It's identity. Here, we can exist, in a space not fully imagined, but once their minds return to this place, we will be gone."

"Right."

"We can only exist in the places they've forgotten. Our external world was colonised centuries ago, given over to the oligarchs. Our internal spaces are being colonised, as well. Our desires, choices, even our memories, poured into the moulds they inscribe."

"So it's their fault we broke into this building?" asked Jack. "Don't think the judge will see it that way."

"Small acts of resistance. Heterogeneity in the face of crushing corporate assimilation."

"Wow. Sounds noble, mate. And complicated. Hetero-what-the-fuck. Shit. Though I got to say: that Chinese woman looked like a large act of resistance, to me."

Col was silent.

"But we nobly stole her shoes instead."

Col just blinked and looked out at the city.

"Fucken revolutionaries, mate."

Col stayed silent, like always when Jack bit back. Preferring the arguments in his own head, the ones he always won.

Jack inhaled deep on the joint to reduce his anger. He let a long cloud trickle from the side of his mouth. "I got an idea where we should go."

"Yeah?"

"Yeah."

"Well?"

Jack wet his lips. "Out of the city. Sleep under the stars."

"Be at one with nature?"

"Um."

"Mosquitoes. Forty-degree heat at five in the morning. Working as indentured labour for some fat-bellied yokel who lets the prettier workers sleep up in his house. That's not our place, Jack. The sunlight would burn us away, we'd disappear. This," said Col, nodding at the view. "This is our universe. You can't escape the universe; you just endure it."

Jack scratched at the scar, the *4007* that'd been carved onto the back of his hand. Held down and cut there. It itched sometimes, in the night air. "I feel like I'll rot, if I stay here."

"Well, that's the universe. Entropy."

"Ah fuck it," said Jack, backhanding Col on the shoulder. "How the fuck can I get high with you around? I'm going to bed."

Col half-smiled, but his mind was already somewhere else.

Jack inhaled a bowl of instant noodles and pulled himself into his sleeping bag. Army surplus. Best investment he'd made in his twenty-two years.

He stared at the ceiling. In that space after consciousness, but before the dreams came, his mind turned over the image of that young Chinese woman. Desperate, sincere in her desperation.

◇

Mid-morning, stomachs empty, they were three blocks from home when the police caught them. Cop car in a near-empty street, parked in the shade of a skyscraper's shell, one officer with his arms crossed, another holding a pulse rifle. Mirrored sunglasses, both.

The first uncrossed his arms. "Jack. Col. Don't even think about running." He took off his shades.

"Officer Bella," said Col. "This isn't your beat."

Mid-thirties, dark eyes, lean. They'd encountered him a few times past couple of years, Jack knew him now. One of those cops who looked like they'd eat your liver, should circumstances allow.

Waves of heat rose from the road, white sun right into their eyes. They eased over to the other side of the road, where a canvas hanging from old scaffolding gave them shade.

Bella stopped two steps from the cruiser, the other cop remained stock-still. The second was big, square-jawed, emotionless. Looked like he belonged in one of those fascist recruiting c-casts the cops had been running lately: *the blue line between order and chaos, the difference is a few good men.*

"I heard you two found yourselves some trouble," said Bella. The sun glinted off the shiny black peak of his hat.

Jack's stomach twisted. He couldn't resist the urge to glance back, at the mouth of an alley. Thin, cop car wouldn't fit, no way. Dark, led to a jungle of rusting scaffolding, chain link fences futilely protecting piles of fine white dirt turning brown, half-imagined new buildings, and mounds of the uncleared rubble of the old.

Bella stepped out to the middle of the road, his oiled boots gleaming, eyes narrowed against the sun. "Been treating our honoured guests with disrespect."

Jack licked his lips. Not the Rebels, then. He drew his intent away from the alley, back to the cop. The woman, Bella knew the woman. But—

"Don't know what you're talking about," said Col.

"Where were you last night, little before midnight?"

"Hmm," Col scratched his chin, feigning an attempt to recollect. "Vinnies soup kitchen down on Albion. Pumpkin, as I recall."

"Got any witnesses?"

Col shrugged, nonchalantly. "How many do you want?"

Bella's face was stone. He stepped into the shadow on Jack and Col's side of the street, his partner shifted the pulse rifle in his arms.

"This is serious. Colin Charles, and you, Jackson Nguyen—" he pinned each with his eyes as he said the names "—have found a kind of trouble way beyond breaking into cars and squatting on building sites. You're going to need to come with us to the station for questioning."

"Of course, officer," said Col.

Bella nodded, once, in satisfaction.

"One thing first, though."

"What?"

"Who's that in the back of the car there?"

Jack looked over at the white-and-blue. Sure enough, through the tinted window, the outline of a third person sitting in the back seat. A black, unmoving outline, watching them.

Bella swallowed. "A detective."

"Name?" asked Col, still feigning everything.

"Not your concern, now—"

"Why so nervous, officer?" asked Col.

Bella took three steps and punched Col in the stomach. So quick all Jack had time to do was stare, open-mouthed, as Col curled into a ball at the feet of the officer. The second cop pointed his pulse rifle at Jack's head.

Bella made a show of loosening the handgun at his hip, resting his hand on the grip. "Listen, you little cunts. You're coming for a ride, and you're going to keep your fucking mouths shut. I don't reckon either of you can afford a dentist. Now—" he reached for his handcuffs.

Jack would rationalise what he did next as one of those out-of-body experiences ice addicts and religious fundamentalists always carped on about. Watching, detached, external, at himself, borderline slow motion.

Bella pulling the stud on the hard leather pouch for the cuffs.

Jack moving so Bella was between him and the second cop, reaching out, hand grasping the grip.

Bella, surprised, frozen for two seconds too long as Jack popped the cop's pistol from its holster.

Calm as Buddha himself, Jack pointing the gun at Bella's head and saying *Move and you're dead, pig.*

The second cop yelling, the back door of the police car popping open, Jack raising his voice and saying it again so everyone heard, everyone believed.

The second cop backing away, not quite knowing what to do with the gleaming pulse rifle.

Jack pulling the trigger, aiming at a point near the second cop's leg. The gun said *click*.

Someone else said: "Let me have that, mate." A friend's voice, speaking through pain. A hand.

Col's hand. It pried the pistol from Jack's.

In his other Col had the snub-nosed revolver resting against Bella's temple. No hesitation, he thumbed the safety on the police-issue and fired three shots at the car.

Jack yelled, ghost returning to body, ears ringing, breathing hard.

Noise, air expelling from the rear tyre of the police car. Bella on the ground two metres away, hands over ears, eyes wild in his head. Second cop gone, third shape no longer there in the back seat.

Col leaned in, his whisper fierce: "Run, *run*."

They fled into the labyrinth.

◇

Baseball caps pulled over their eyes, they walked in a part of town they weren't used to: a rich part. Col had insisted; his fence for the shoes lived nearby, above an organic wine bar. Police-issue pistol long gone, thrown away as they ran from the scene. GPS trackers in its bullets, in every component, the hottest and the worst thing a crook could hold on to.

Col had sold the woman's shoes, part money, part trade for some second-hand clothes rich people'd pay ten times the price for if you called them *vintage* instead of *second-hand*. They'd asked for face masks, but the fence said, no, didn't have any, and they were out of fashion anyway. Instead he gave them two voluminous scarves, black and purple, dully shimmering, vaguely ridiculous. *In fashion*, the fence had said. Jack had hoped for a decent pair of boots in the mix, but what they got instead was faded jeans, white shirts, red sneakers, weird-smelling denim jackets. The fence, sharp-featured, eyes-darting, one hand resting on top of the other, halo of black-grey hair, called them ironic. Said no-one would recognise them.

Jack didn't know how irony worked as a disguise, but it worked. They walked down Chapel Street. Past cafés filled with massively muscled men, arms and necks writhing with tattoos, drinking elderflower tea from tiny glass cups, talking skin care and resorts.

And women, blonde. Jack couldn't tell them apart. High heels, muscled calves, power jackets, briefcases, angry.

Chinese, too, students, children of the red aristocracy, bearing Dolce & Gabbana or Fujian original purses like totems, like shields.

Jack and Col walked among them, heads down. Facial recognition cameras on every street, the duo wore the large sunglasses that were fortuitously in fashion with men. Walking funny – Col had made Jack put a rock in the heel of his shoe. Some surveillance tech could pick up a unique gait. Police could use the on-retina feeds of regular citizens as well, to find suspects. If they had a warrant, if it was serious enough.

They'd shot at cops. Pretty serious.

They avoided eye contact. Scarves up, faces down. Best way to avoid surveillance tech was to not look at it. Old school.

Their mouths watered. At the real coffee, the real meat, the large-lipped women, and the soft-skinned men who'd crumple in a fight. They walked through longing to eat, drink, fight, and fuck. But they didn't have enough money for that, not in this part of town.

Jack paused among the tables of an outdoor café. A group of white-teethed patrons had just left, half-eaten salads, fries, tempeh on their plates. He glanced around, under the peak of his cap. No waiters present. He'd taken two steps before Col's hand found his upper arm, pulled him away, dragged him between shopfronts to an alley.

"Don't be fucken stupid," said Col.

"I'm hungry."

"Same here. But we can't draw attention."

"There's money left over. Let's buy something."

Col shook his head. "Not here. Too expensive. We need the cash."

"We need to go get our stuff."

"No."

"Yes."

"We go back," said Col, "we die. I can feel it, Jack. Death is waiting there, for us."

"Fuck that druggo talk," said Jack, angry, stomach gnawing, mouth parched. The alley smelled of garbage, fermenting in the heat. "We got to run? We'll need our food, our sleeping bags. We need to make money? My tools are there. And that flexiscreen – we'll get a thousand bucks for that. They don't know where we're staying, Col – how could they? We walk there, no trams, no transit ID. Early morning, we get our shit and split. Hang out down the uni, look for some kids leaving by car, need to split the recharge bill for the ride. Fuck—" Jack pulled at his shirt "—we look like fucking students now."

"I can't leave."

"We got no choice, mate."

"It won't let me leave, Jack. The city will punish me if I try."

"*Motherfucker*," said Jack, voice raised. They both glanced back towards the alley mouth. No-one was there, no-one noticed. Jack lowered it: "What? Fucken voodoo? Then where? Then how?"

"Poorer suburb, trailer park maybe."

"With what money?"

"From the shoes, with what we can steal. We can manage."

"Yeah," said Jack. "Maybe. But for that we'll need to sell what we got back at the building site."

"Listen—"

"No. I'm done listening to your space cadet bullshit. You want to hide among the bogans? Fine. I get it. They're our people. But we won't hold a trailer two weeks without decent cash and a way to make more. No more spirit-talk, fuck-knuckle, *we get our shit.*"

Col was silent. Not used to Jack stringing so many words together, nor to him having a strong opinion on much at all. Col stepped away, leaned against the wall, eyes somewhere over Jack's shoulder. His lips moved, speaking to himself.

Ten feet down from them, an iron door opened. A man stepped out holding a black guitar case in hand, and a spare tyre – including gleaming rims – in the other.

Jack sighed and stepped back, letting the man walk between him and Col. Jack pulled a cigarette from his pocket and leaned against the opposite wall of the alley. Lit the smoke, inhaled deep, taking pleasure in the pain of the smoke as it bit his lungs.

Col said, eventually, softly: "That Chinese woman. She pulled us into her world."

The Chinese woman. Begging, beautiful, vulnerable, untouchable. If Jack could just get her name—

Jack was about to reply when a glowing red message appeared on-retina: *Warning – you are not allowed to smoke within fifty metres of a restaurant, café, bar, or betting agency within the City limits.* FINE: FIVE THOUSAND DOLLARS.

A pause, and then the words:

The City cannot read your cochlear-glyph implant. Please remain where you are until a Parks and Gardens representative can arrive in person and issue your fine.

"Fuck," said Jack. He chucked his cigarette, turned, and ran down the alley with Col.

◇

Yao Li followed the spore, superimposed on-retina. Pulled from police files, the DNA signatures of Colin Charles and Jackson Nguyen were easy to track. Not many traversed the streets of the restricted construction zone, and these two kids were degenerates and petty bandits: they had not the skills nor the tech nor the money to hide themselves.

Yao Li had felt a tic of irritation when given the assignment. But that tic stayed far beneath the surface. Nothing, but nothing, came anywhere near the unbroken surface of his pond.

Instead, he simply nodded after the upstart executive had given the order. Thirty years old and already treating Yao with disdain – dispensing with formalities, not even offering tea when he had entered the office. Sixty storeys up, plush red carpet, a painting of Confucius in a heavy gold frame on one wall, and views out over the city. The executive had given him the task bluntly, staring at him through superfluous steel-rimmed spectacles. Two boys who knew too much, loose ends. Yao Li bowed and left.

Four years in this city at the end of the world, at the periphery of anything that mattered, for taking out the wrong man in Macau. One of their own, a Sinopec senior executive. As punishment they'd sent him, their best, to a city that could fall off the face of the Earth unnoticed and unmourned by the rest of humanity.

Yao Li had not killed the wrong man. He'd killed precisely the right one: a middle-aged and arrogant former military officer, assassinated on the whim of a young and ambitious princeling from the red aristocracy. A business rival dispensed with, an undignified act caused by an uneven temperament. But Yao Li was loyal to the family of the princeling, so he had done as ordered. His reward was not a firing squad, but rather exile.

Just a few months, they'd told him.

Now four years. Yao would have preferred the firing squad.

Yao Li bypassed the lock to the building in eight seconds, ghosted up the forty-eight storeys in under six minutes. At the top, breathing even, not a bead of sweat.

Head to toe, shadow black, unseen as he drifted through a large open office space, teeming with DNA. Sound: snoring, gentle, next room. Yao's carbon alloy hand, sleek, matte black, eased the needle pistol from the holster at the small of his back. Each needle had neurotoxins enough to kill a large man twice over.

The chest of the boy rose and fell, rose and fell. Lying, fully clothed, red sneakers on his feet, mouth parted, vivid purple scar across his cheek. Stillness. Water dripping from a tap in the next room. Wind caressing the building.

Yao Li, black on black, noiseless, watching.

He raised the pistol and fired two shots: neck and ear. The boy's eyes popped open, his mouth gasped for breath. The boy turned his head towards Yao Li.

Yao blinked, surprised he had been able to move at all. Loss of all muscle control, instantaneous, then death, were the only aftereffects. The eyes came to rest on Yao Li, sheathed in the dark, yet still the eyes sought and saw the assassin. Stared right into him, eyes glazing, then glazed, then looking at nothing at all.

Yao looked away, inscribing a ward in the air with his human hand. His shadow parted from wall shadow. To the stairs, soundless. His ears had picked out and isolated relevant noises two floors above: shoes scuffing on plascrete, the click of a cigarette lighter, a long inhalation of breath.

He glided up, out onto the roof. Yao Li paused, listened to the Milky Way as it flowed across the sky. It was bright up top, stars shimmering, the boy sitting on the edge of the building, looking out at the city. Smoking a cigarette, book resting on the ledge, next to him.

Yao Li pulled the black, leather-bound handle from his belt. He clicked the recessed button near the hilt and the blade materialised. A black, gleaming, nano-sharpened edge, curved. He stepped forwards, his dao sword pointed at the back of the sitting boy. Fast, he decided, between the ribs, into the heart, painless. Dead before the awareness of that fact reached his brain.

The boy blew a cloud of smoke into the air, while the wind sang through steel construction cables. Three metres away, moving, Li pulled back the blade.

A second person came at him from the right, peripheral, completely silent. Yao hissed and turned, defensive pose. He had detected nothing – no sound or movement – but still he'd come, a figure swathed in shadow like Li, its pale white face floating above darkness. No-one, in more than a decade, had got the drop on Yao Li.

Nothing, nothing was there. Yao Li spun, heart beating fast, and spun again, but still nothing. Just rough plascrete, unfinished wind turbines, and the first drops of rain.

Someone said *fuck*.

Yao Li turned again, and Jackson Nguyen was looking at him, eyes wide, a revolver in his hand.

◇

Jack stared at the killer. Barely visible all in black, but the blade it held shone under the distant city lights. Its eyes shone as well, with an intent that was absolutely clear.

In Jack's hand, the gun. The one Col had bought a box of untracked bullets for earlier that day, from the fence.

He didn't think. He just squeezed the trigger.

The killer grunted and moved, a blur, right at Jack.

Jack stepped back, firing again, wild, tripped, fell backwards. He grasped for an edge, for anything, but found only air. A long second of empty space, wind rushing past his ears, until he crashed into something hard. He groaned, blood on his lip, looked up on instinct. Only blackness above, but he was sure the killer was there, watching, aiming.

Jack had fallen ten feet to their third security measure. A construction platform, one metre wide, three long, cabled from top to bottom of the skyscraper. One of a number of temporary, open-air elevators attached to the side of the building.

Jack slammed the control panel with his palm, the floor gave way underneath him. Only ever meant for escape, Jack had programmed it to drop, stone cold, with gravity, before a graduated slowdown over the last two floors.

He gasped, the air lifting his clothes and hair, the only sounds the screeching of cables and the bellowing of the wind. Hoping, praying he'd rigged it right, that it would work.

It worked. More or less.

Screaming the last few metres, sparks flying, Jack gripped the railing like it was the hand of god. His torso whiplashed, the lift stop-starting the last few feet. Instinct, only instinct, drove him on. He flopped over the rail into the dirt. Rain getting heavier, big fat drops. Revolver long gone, flung into the abyss.

Stumbling and falling, palms scraped, back on his feet. Jack staggered out to the street, rain beating harder, first wet in months. Dry earth drinking it in, steel and asphalt and plascrete roaring in pleasure as the rain beat down *beat down*.

Jack stopped on the road, trying to get his bearings, wiping water from his face with his forearm. Someone whispered, close, mouth right at his ear: *he's coming.* Jack spun and spun again, hands up, ready to punch and tear. Nothing. He blinked. Empty streets, road slick with water, blue neon beer signs. *Run* whispered the voice, fierce, familiar. Jack took two steps onto the road, spinning, stumbling. *RUN*, it yelled.

He ran.

Right down the centre of the street. Fear propelling him, in the open, no thought to turn or hide. Heart pounding in his chest, scream tearing against the back of his throat, some sublime terror rising within, a subterranean instinct, knowing, knowing, death was stalking.

◇

Sage Campbell drove down Rutland, fast. Late to work, again, taking a short cut through the construction zone. One more warning away from the sack. The company wanted to replace the last of the truckies with auto-driven rigs, but the union had won a rare victory, guaranteeing jobs until the driver voluntarily left or was fired. So the company, the sons-of-bitches, took any infraction they could find to knife the working man. Get them off the books, replace them with an automaton designed by some silver-spoon fuckwit from Zhongguancun. *Driverless vehicles are one hundred per cent safe*, these cunts said. Bullshit. More like no holidays, no sick leave, no fucking pay claims, ever.

He made a hard left. Horses all a wash – his *sure thing* ended up with a nice view of the field, crossing the finish line three lengths behind second last place. Few beers as a consolation, no harm in that. But one minute late or thirty, these bastards didn't care: all they wanted was him gone.

Rain hammering the windshield, wipers on full, truck humming, warm in the cab. A couple of long blinks, shake of the head. Tired. Long day in the sun at the races.

Sage spun the wheel again, took the hill at pace down Harrow. Streets wet and deserted, the wind whipping the rain. He eased up on the accelerator as he sailed into the next, turning the wheel into the right—

—at a man, standing in the road, an apparition. Young man, body in shadow, pale face, white face, vivid purple scar, staring right into the headlights—

—Sage swore and yanked the wheel away, straightening, brake pedal smashed to the floor, *FUUUUUUUCK*—

◇

Yao Li ran, free flowing, despite the hole in his lung. In spite of it. On-retina, his combat medical system reported clottocyte nanos had amped up the coagulation, stopped the bleeding. Pumped painkillers enough to ease the piercing agony in his chest, upped the adrenaline. It made him feel uncomfortably close to euphoric. A gunshot high, he'd heard it called.

He hurdled a fluoro-orange construction barricade, winced as he landed, but continued his rhythmic, practised stride. It was the first time Li had been shot and the shame of it burned harder than the bullet. By the hand of a petty brigand. His exile was perhaps deserved, after all.

A truck rumbled in the distance; he filtered out the noise. His heightened senses picked up footsteps ahead, DNA spore all over the road. A vagrant and a bandit, yet Yao had exposed himself, had allowed…

He set his jaw. Yao Li would take this boy's head. Clean the skull. Place it in his vault.

The white static of the rain was filtered out by his hearing, allowing him to pinpoint the *splash splash splash* of his target, running. A few per cent of infrared into his vision, and the outline of the boy was clear, a hundred metres up the road. Yao Li ate up the distance between them easily, stride strong, ignoring the rain that battered his face, the tightness in his side.

The needle pistol was in his hand again, arm out, horizontal, perfectly steady.

Headlights lit up the road ahead of him. The truck was turning down his street. Yao Li, focused on his prey, ignored the vehicle as it bent into a turn. The boy's back a wide, easy target.

The truck, angling away from him, swerved suddenly.

The scream of brakes, Yao's infra-filter blinding as the high beams lit him up. His foot slipped, teeth gritted, he leapt.

◇

Jack turned at the blast of the horn.

The image imprinted: the killer, black silhouette in the beams of the truck, forward-flipping out of its path, high and free of impact.

Almost. Until ankle clipped.

The body spun in the air, a stick broken and thrown. The truck fishtailed, its driver forcing an impossible angle on the steering wheel, the rear back corner swinging around and swatting the spinning shadow a second time, propelling it across the wet road, over the gutter, flip-flop rag doll, propped against the wall.

The truck slammed through a construction barricade, crushed a low brick wall, shuddered to a halt. The driver's cab door flew open. A middle-aged man with lank hair and a large stomach jumped out, eyes wide staring at a spot on the street. He swore.

Jack walked back through the rain, breathing heavy, road surface glistening in the streetlights. Neural pinged Col. Silence.

The driver saw Jack approach. "Did you see the other man?" he asked. "The one I missed?" He looked around, frantic. A man with a tenuous grip on a mortgage, a family, a life – that slender thread taut, about to snap.

Jack walked right past him. Wiping the rain from his eyes with the back of his sleeve, he stepped up to the shadow creature. It was small, surprisingly small. A Chinese male. Only five feet tall. Body broken, eyes calm, fixed on Jack, still alive, utterly devoid of emotion.

Jack bent down, picked up a metallic-blue needle pistol from the ground. The killer groaned, his body shifted, but that was all. Legs shattered, sticking out at obscene angles, his blood pooling on the slick plascrete.

Jack straightened, turned the weapon over in his hands. Over his shoulder, he heard the *plop plop plop* as the driver turned and ran into the rain.

He said: "I reckon this'd be untracked and undocumented. No doubt about it."

The small man in black said nothing.

The pistol shone in Jack's hand. He looked for and found the safety, clicked it, and pointed the gun at the man's head.

"Why?" he asked.

The man seemed to smile at that, the corner of his mouth twitching upwards.

"I guess you're the type of man who'd never talk," said Jack, quietly.

The man didn't talk.

"It's that woman, isn't it? You all think there's some grand conspiracy. That she gave us something important maybe. Told us something. We just stole her shoes: did you know that?"

That twitch-smile at the corner of the assassin's mouth again. But still, he said nothing.

"You're gonna die, mate. So may as well give it up, what was this all about?"

The Chinese man opened his mouth, his lips glistened with blood. In Mandarin, he said: "[All of life is a dream walking. Death is going home.]"

"Yeah," said Jack as the translation came through. "Yeah, I figured. More fucken voodoo. No straight lines in this city."

Jack sighed. He'd never know. He'd never come close to knowing. Instead, he said: "Tell me this, then – did you kill Col?"

The killer nodded, no hesitation.

Jack nodded back and shot a needle into the man's face. Then a second. Then a third. The killer lost all muscle control, face twisting in on itself, mouth popping eyeball popping, something guttural came from the man's throat. Then he was gone.

Jack looked down at the body. Slowly, he went to one knee. Then both. His hands flopped down onto his thighs, the pistol clattering onto the road. His body shook, starting from the chest. A pain buried deep there, shaking his whole frame as it came loose.

"Motherfucker," croaked Jack, through tears.

He'd known before the man had replied. Known Col was dead. Jackson Nguyen looked out at the neon shining up from the darkling earth. At the city of ghosts, both dead and living. Col with them now, always with them. Ghosts to history, ghosts to the present, moving through the shadows of the world. The universe.

He felt the city reach out and embrace him with its vast indifference.

◇

Sally Redacre walked from her last lecture, elated. The semester was done. Her subjects all passed. The parents and their six-hundred grand tuition fee, temporarily placated. Out into the baking car park, she paused and looked for the guy – Jack something – who had answered her uninet message about the car share.

She was a little surprised to see the guy waiting near her ride. She didn't recall telling him what she drove.

He was in his early twenties, denim on denim, with a cigarette in his hand. Asian, Chinese maybe. Too thin, but handsome, trying to hide it under a Melbourne Storm cap, pulled down low. But his eyes twinkled, his jaw strong.

"You can't smoke in the car," she said, annoyed, surprised. She'd never met anyone who smoked.

He dropped the cigarette and crushed it under his red sneaker.

She raised an eyebrow at that, but also noticed the rolled-up sleeping bag and backpack at his feet. The graphic novel sitting on top reassured her, somehow. After an awkward silence she said: "Well, um, Jack. I got your credit transfer, thanks."

Jack scratched the back of his hand. Sally couldn't help but notice a rough tattoo of the number *4007* there. It looked deliberately distressed, she supposed in line with the latest fashion.

"What a lovely tattoo," she said, still attempting conversation. "Does that number have some special meaning to you?"

He pulled his sleeve so it re-covered the tat and said, in a broad Australian accent: "Yeah. It's the amount I once owed to bookies down in Geelong. They put it there as a reminder."

She took the deadpan delivery as dry humour and laughed. "Well, I suppose we should be going. You have family in Perth?"

"Not yet."

She took this as more humour, smiling. "Ha. Well, let's get going then."

"Yeah," he agreed, his hand on top of the car, looking back at the city. He seemed to be listening to something and for a moment, floating on the breeze, Sally thought she heard someone whistling classical music.

"Yeah," he said again. "It's time I left."

PART TWO

A Vast Silence

"...their constant language was, an apprehension of the impracticability of returning home, the dread of a sickly passage, and the fearful prospect of a distant and barbarous country."

Watkin Tench, A Narrative of the Expedition to Botany Bay (1789)

The police caught them a hundred kilometres into the Nullarbor Plain. Blue lights flashing, Jackson Nguyen's knuckles white on the dashboard. Sally Redacre moved her sunglasses up to the top of her head, pushing back her long fringe. "Oh. Did I do something?"

The blue lights turned. Good cop/flash/bad cop/flash. Could be either.

Bad cop, said the ghost inside his head.

"Were you speeding, Sally?" asked Jack, his voice even.

She glanced between him and the rear-view mirror. Blonde hair, blue eyes. Sally Redacre was wealthy, kind, and possessed of a brand of unadorned beauty Jack associated with women who'd grown up on healthy diets and supportive families. Which meant he'd resented her from the moment they'd met in the uni car park back in Melbourne. Prejudice, rising unbidden. He'd sat in the passenger's seat for the first few hours of the trip, unresponsive to her polite conversation, mind swirling around what he'd left behind. To the body at the construction site, twice shot with a needle pistol.

Turned himself from the young woman's words and stared out at the world as it passed by. The sun-flattened streets of suburb and outer-suburb, as the noise and the fury of the city were left behind. Melbourne: teeming, frenetic, the only home he ever knew, only place he'd ever lived. As the city and its satellites fell behind, his gnawing detachment turned to wonder. The vastness of it all, the neon gods of Melbourne long forgotten, like they never existed. The sleeping giant of the land made the city seem so small, its concerns so distant.

◇

At the edge of the Nullarbor Plain, they'd stopped to recharge Sally's red Tesla Ganymede at a battery station, field of panels behind, glinting in the sunlight. Sally had gone to the bathroom and left him in blessed silence. When he'd stepped out into the open air, an immense quiet had weighed down on him. Nothing, but the *tic-tic-tic* of the charger, and the sigh of the car on baking asphalt.

Quiet, until a voice said: *Drive.*

Jack, reverie gone, snapped his head around.

Drive, the voice said again. Urging. Jack swore and shook his head.

"Everything okay?" Sally asked, suddenly there, next to him. Straw fedora on her head.

"Do you hear that?"

"Hear what?"

"Nothing." Jack scratched at the rough tattoo carved into the back of his hand. "I just want to keep moving."

"Yes," said Sally, turning her eyes to the far horizon. The cochlear-glyph implant behind her ear glinted in the light. "It's the third time I've made this drive," she continued. "All day and all night, and nothing changes. Just red earth and salt bush. After a while it feels like a dream, it's… it's maddening in a way. You start to doubt yourself, begin to wonder if you're hallucinating." She waited, shutting up for a change, and smiled at him. It was a quiet smile. Despite himself, his resentments wavered. "It's stupid," she finished.

"Nah," said Jack. He pulled a soft pack of cigarettes from his pocket, tapped one out. "This is stupid."

"Honestly, you're the first person I've ever met who smokes."

He lit up. "You're the first I've met who drives."

She raised her eyebrows. "Driving doesn't kill you."

"That ain't true at all."

"Well. Maybe. But smoking's another thing entirely."

"I'll get lung rejuv."

"Will you? Got a spare ten million lying around?"

"Can't you tell?" Jackson spread his arms wide, indicating his attire.

"You've had the same shirt on for two days."

"Two weeks."

"Ew."

"Maid took a break."

"Hmm. I wanted to ask you something."

"Yeah?"

"Do you…?"

Jackson smoked.

"Are you…?"

He wiped the sweat from his brow with the back of his hand. "Bloody hell. Spit it out."

"Are you between apartments at the moment?"

Sally was acting pretty decent, given she was worried she'd picked up a vagrant. "Yeah," he lied. "New one after this holiday."

"Oh," she said, so relieved she didn't think to interrogate his answer further. "So many students are in a difficult situation these days. The tent city down on the South Lawn is a disgrace."

"Yeah." Jack felt a flash of pride at the thought that she thought he could be at uni. Then he remembered he'd hacked the university intranet and masqueraded as a student to get a ride-share. Sally'd put a post up asking for a fellow student to split the costs. So yeah, course she thought that.

Someone whispered at the back of his mind. Caught on the breeze from he knew not where. Nothing out here but the ghost of a dead friend. A trick of the conscience, chipping away at reason. Jack crushed his cigarette, half-finished, underfoot and said: "Let's go."

◇

"I can't have been speeding," said Sally, looking down at the dashboard. "The car wouldn't let me."

He squinted out the rear window, at the two cops exiting the police cruiser. The figures' black silhouettes against the white of the sun. As they approached, a third figure, not in uniform, emerged from the back of the car.

Bad cop, whispered a voice. His voice. Col Charles. A dead man, talking.

Sally told the car to lower the driver's side window. A female cop's face appeared in the space, black hair tied back, eyes hidden behind mirrored sunglasses. On the other side, the second officer – big guy, shirt stretched tight across his broad chest, hand resting on his holstered pistol – approached Jack's window.

Bad cops, Col said, urgently.

"What seems to be the problem, Officer?" asked Sally, smiling, polite. Civilian, right side of the thin blue line, ever helpful.

"Retina scan, champ," the female officer replied. Jack couldn't be sure, what with the sunglasses, but it felt like she was looking at him.

"Oh," replied Sally. "Of course." She leaned forwards, chin up, ready for the scan.

Four things happened quickly:

The female cop pulled back her elbow and rammed the black metal scanner against Sally's forehead.

The burly cop on Jackson's side pulled the pistol from his holster.

The voice inside Jack's head screamed *DRIVE*.

Jack ducked and slammed his hand down on the accelerator.

Then three more things happened:

The car hummed forwards.

The back windshield exploded.

And Sally screamed.

Jackson, chest across her thighs, yelled up at her: "Steer it, steer!"

The car wobbled but the wheels turned, wind whistling through the holes in the front windscreen. Jack managed to crane his neck and look up at Sally. Eyes wide, trickle of blood down the centre of her forehead. She was taking shallow breaths, falling into shock.

"Can you drive?" he yelled over the wind.

Unblinking, breathing *huh-huh-huh*, unaware of the man across her lap. Jack swore and grabbed her sneakered foot, manoeuvred it over the accelerator, and pressed it down. When he was sure she was going to keep it down, he raised himself back up. Blue lights flashing behind, wind whipping at his hair, fear firmly wrapped around his heart.

The bitumen arrow of the road, arcing beyond the curvature of the Earth. A sign, not so far back, had announced: *90 Mile Straight. Australia's Longest Straight Road. 146.6 KM.* Jack had instigated the most boring car chase in history. Most predictable, as well: Civilian cars were programmed to max out at one hundred klicks, cop cars at one-fifty. So the cops gained ground and Jack swore and Sally displayed all the getaway driving skills of a corpse. Pressed back into her chair, rigid, unblinking.

Turn right, two kilometres.

"There's a right turn comin' up!" yelled Jack, over the wind. Sally said nothing, lucid-dreaming her life.

One kilometre.

Jack could see the shapes in the car, silhouettes three, as the cruiser ate up the bitumen behind. Warning lights bleeped on the dashboard. The voice of the car, monotone, announced: "I have received a cease-engine notice from the Australian Federal Police. Car will halt in thirty seconds."

"Fuck," spat Jack.

Turn, said the ghost.

Jack ripped the wheel from Sally, her hands popping off it as the car's tyres squealed, squeal turning to a roar as they hit a red dirt road running at a right angle to the main. Rock and dust flew up behind them and the car counted down: "Thirty, twenty-nine, twenty-eight—"

He risked a glance back – the cop car overshot the turn, fishtailing to a stop.

"—twenty, nineteen, eighteen—"

The road weaved in and out of the salt scrub sprinkled across the desert's face, leading to no particular place Jack could determine. No township no signs no other vehicles.

"—six, five, four—"

The car slowed to a quiescent stop. Jack popped the door, cloud of dust billowing inwards. He made to get out but Sally, zombie no more, had his sleeve. "Don't leave me!"

"You'll be safe." He pulled his arm from hers roughly. "They're after me."

"What did you do?"

"You'll be fine."

Run, Jack, run.

Through tears and snot and blood, she cried, "They hit me. *They hit me.*"

She had a point. Still, he backed away from her; she held out her hand, like a scared child to a parent.

She'll be fine.

Jack ran. A familiar sickness tore at him, his soul in revolt at his cowardice.

He'd made it six steps before someone yelled: "Freeze!" Three more before the pulse arc hit him.

◇

Jackson Nguyen groaned. The aftertaste of metal and dirt in his mouth. He tried to push himself up, but found his arms were pinned behind his back. *Clink clink.* Handcuffed.

A woman's voice. "Okay, champ. Let's get you the fuck up." Rough hands dragged him to his feet.

Another voice. Not rough. Smooth, like the surface of a frozen pond, said, "Thank you, Officer Stebbins. I shall question the suspect."

"Yes, sir," said the woman, her tone changed completely. Footsteps, fading.

Hands manoeuvred Jack to a low, flat boulder facing the setting sun, and sat him down. Jack's ribs hurt. His jeans were covered in dust.

The man in charge sat next to him. He was some kind of apparition. Like a hologram, untouched by the landscape, no dust on his polished black shoes, no sweat on his forehead. Neat part in his dark hair, no sunglasses, no hat. Pulse pistol, badge shining on his belt. He smelled of cologne, though too much. Jack turned and spat to get the taste of it out of his mouth.

The man turned his dark, shining eyes on him. Fear touched the back of Jack's neck. "Detective Quinlan. Good to meet you finally, Mr Nguyen."

Hit him.

Jack said nothing while the eyes stayed on him. Then the man in the fine suit turned to the horizon. But the echoes of Quinlan's eyes remained in the space between them, like the Cheshire cat. No smile, though. Jack blinked the illusion away.

Hit him, said his ghost. The other illusion. The real one.

"The voice," said Jack, "Can you hear it?"

The burnt-orange hue of the sunset reflected on the detective's face. "I hear nothing," said Quinlan, not missing a beat. "Because there's nothing to hear, Mr Nguyen. Just the great silence of this land as it sleeps. Like the kraken. The silence of its slumber pressing down on us all. An oppression. But when it wakes, then you will hear it. And it will be the last thing you hear."

Jack paused for a moment after the soliloquy. "The fuck? You auditioning for community theatre, mate?"

"It is wise to fear this land," said Quinlan, oblivious. "Though right now this sentiment should not take precedence. Now you should fear the man beside you, with a gun and the willingness to use it."

Jack said nothing to that, turned instead to look at the same thing the detective was looking at. It stilled him. His heart, trying to force its way out of his chest. The futile backchat on the tip of his tongue. His breathing settled, and so the silence fell on him as well, physical.

After a time, Quinlan said, "The Chinese woman gave you something. We would like it back, Mr Nguyen."

Jack cleared his throat. "Cigarette."

"She gave you cigarettes?"

Jack shook his head. "My right pocket."

"Ah. Well, consider it the carrot, Mr Nguyen. We are both well aware of the stick. The woman?"

"Nice pair of real leather high heels."

"Excuse me?"

"The Chinese bird. Shoes. Don't reckon they'd fit you, though."

"I see. I find it pleasing to meet someone who still retains a spirit, Mr Nguyen. Most I encounter are sallow and long corrupted. Like the two officers who accompanied me here. Two among so many, lean and hungry, waiting in underfunded stations, adrift in the sea of scum produced by our cities." Still he looked at the horizon. "I could throw her to them like a piece of meat, Mr Nguyen. Your girlfriend, Miz Redacre. They would defile her, willingly and at length."

Hit this ponderous cunt. Run towards the riverbed.

Jack couldn't see a riverbed. Just the desert, stretching out to eternity. Quinlan's dark eyes swam in the last of the sun's rays. The land, silent, listened to the two men sitting atop it.

"I don't know her," said Jack.

"No?"

"I met her yesterday. She thinks I'm a uni student."

"The facts of the case are yet to be established, Mr Nguyen. Until you prove to me otherwise, she shall be considered an accomplice." Quinlan paused. "The extraction of this information is as inevitable as the setting sun."

Run.

"In fact, let's make it the sunset. Before it dips below the horizon you will talk, or your girlfriend will suffer." Detective Quinlan continued to watch the goddamn horizon. The only indication he was giving any thought to Jack were the words coming out of his mouth. Every other part of the man's attention elsewhere.

Run.

Jack winced at the voice in his head. Familiar, unfamiliar. Alien and unwelcome, his closest friend, one week dead. Col, alive again, haunting him, insistent.

"But the girl," he said, to Col.

"Don't worry about the woman," replied the detective.

Don't worry about the woman.

Jack sighed. Tensed his shoulders and leaned his body forwards, pressure building on the balls of his feet. Quinlan didn't notice.

Jack rammed the top of his head into the side of the detective's. Jack staggered, stinging-ringing with pain, slipped to one knee, planted his other foot, heaved himself up, and ran. One glance back: Quinlan, toppled, hair mussed, mouth agape as he tried to push himself up.

Jack ran across the red dirt, bent at the waist, arms cuffed behind him.

Somewhere, doors slammed. Silence no more as his heart pounded in his ears. His ankle twisted and he fell—

Into the shadows of the riverbed, appearing from nowhere. He tasted dirt again. Something popped and whirred. A bullet, but far away. Jack rolled, heaved himself up, and ran and ran, shadows everywhere, sun setting fast. Mind turning to the girl, behind, what they would do to her. No sound of pursuit. No more bullets. Just Jack's breathing, ragged, and a voice at the centre of his mind, like a fitness coach for his cowardice, urging him to *run run run.*

◇

A shadow flitted around the corner, footfalls pounding, Jack pulled back his blade, too late, the body colliding with his. He lost balance, fell, his knife skittering on the concrete.

When he got to his knees, Col was pointing his gun at the woman while she spoke rapid-fire in Mandarin, palms open in surrender, also on her knees.

Jack's cochlear implant translated the words, two seconds after they left her mouth.

[. . . soon. Money, I can give you money if you help me. I work for bleeeep.*]*

◇

Jack woke, senses blurred. Face hovering above him, a silhouette against the white heat.

It's okay, mate. You're safe now.

"Do you hear the voice? Do you hear it?" Jack said, words slurred.

"Yeah, brother," replied the silhouette. "Of course I hear them."

Jack's mind swayed, his consciousness failed to put its fragments together.

◇

[I came here t-to meet a man from The Age. *Reveal the truth about the next generation AI. The Profurn Affair.]*

Col licked his lips, unusually lost for words, and glanced back towards the street, people bustling past in the light. He said: "Hmm. Bleep. *Sounds serious."*

She looked confused. Even in the dim alley. Her confusion, the fear that tightened her jaw, were clear.

Col continued, "If it's serious enough for my translator to censor it, then you have a problem no amount of lucre can fix, especially by two petty crooks."

◇

The man awoke, arm stretched back behind his head. The waking man looked at the ceiling, white paint peeling from metal. Cool, in the space. He thought about walking into town, getting hot chips and a cold beer at the Ace in the Hole pub on Barkly Street. Watching the pedestrians, worker bees in their fine civvies, buzzing back and forth. He thought about washing his jeans and spare shirt at the coin laundry, giving Sally a call. She had this quiet smile, you see. Something in it.

Jackson Nguyen winced as he remembered where and who and what. All the possibilities that existed in those sweet seconds of amnesia after waking, disappeared. The world rushed back in and Jack could only be one thing. Was only ever one thing. Predestined.

"You're awake, brother."

Jack started, worked himself to a sitting position. His arm didn't obey instruction – he found it handcuffed to a metal leg of a work desk next to the couch.

An Indigenous man sat across from him in a cracked faux-leather armchair that matched the one Jack was in. The slender man wore tan slacks, a pressed long-sleeve shirt, and a distinguished salt-and-pepper beard. One leg crossed over the other at a right angle, flexiscreen green-glowing in his lap. They were in a demountable, Jack assumed, a glorified shipping container ten metres by about three. Couches at this end, workstation at the other, maps over the walls outlining topography and borders of some kind, light too bright through the windows to tell what was outside.

"Where am I?" croaked Jack.

"Furnace Range."

The man studied him. Jack couldn't find anything in his gaze. Not anger, or suspicion, nothing. Whatever the man's opinion, it was too far in the distance to imprint on Jack.

"Water."

The other man indicated the bench next to Jack. On it were his cigarettes and a paper cup filled with water. Jack reached out and downed it in one go, gasping.

"Dehydrated, mate," said the other man. "Out all night and all day."

Jack picked up his smokes. "You mind?"

The man indicated for him to proceed. Jack grabbed the pack, extracted a cigarette with his lips.

"Jack."

"Charlie."

Jack patted his pockets. "Damn. Got a light?"

The man placed the screen on the desk next to him and rose from his chair. That's when Jack saw the gun. And the badge. He froze. The cop saw it all; Jack knew it, the cop knew it. He lit the cigarette anyway and sat back down. Jack sucked in the smoke but the bite in his lungs didn't satisfy, didn't unbind the knot in his guts.

"Cheers," said Jack.

Charlie waited.

Jack exhaled a cloud of smoke. "What's next, Officer?"

The other man indicated the flexiscreen next to him with a tilt of his head. A green light pulsed on the display. "You get picked up. Again."

"The cops coming, they're corrupt."

Charlie watched him.

"They've set me up."

"It's like you mob get together, practise your denials."

"I'm not a criminal."

"Record says otherwise."

Jack leaned forwards, his head swimming from the sudden movement. "Shit. Yeah. Okay. I'm a crim. Petty, as the record will also say. But the main cop coming, Quinlan – he's going to kill us."

"I know who Hank Quinlan is. One of the most decorated officers in the Australian Federal Police."

The voice whispered to him. Jack listened.

Jack asked, "Did Quinlan put out a general bulletin on my escape? Or was there a message to you direct?"

Charlie creased his brow. "How did you know to ask that?"

"Is it standard procedure?"

"I asked you a question."

"The voice in my head told me."

Charlie looked back at the flexiscreen. "You have several hacking convictions."

"Fuck. I override security systems at vacant buildings so I can have a dry place to sleep. I haven't suddenly graduated to hacking the internal comms system of the AFP, mate."

They have to kill Charlie.

"What?" asked Jack, tilting his head to one side.

They will kill you and Sally, which means they have to kill Charlie. That's why they sent out an alert to this settlement only. Charlie can't see you alive, only for you to turn up dead later.

"Voice again?" asked Charlie.

"They're going to kill you," said Jack.

Charlie's eyes flashed. "Listen, mate. They'll be here in five minutes. I don't want to hear any more of your bullshit."

"There's a woman with me. Innocent. Knows too much. If they kill her, they have to kill you. You're the only witness."

Charlie stood. "Turn around."

"I—"

"Turn around!" Charlie yelled, in his cop voice. Jack shut up and did what he was told. The officer uncuffed him from the table, twisted Jack's arms behind his back, and re-clicked the handcuffs firm.

Jack squinted at the heat and light as he walked down the three metal stairs of the demountable. Then he stopped. Despite it all, the fury and fear running through his head, he stopped cold.

Five metres away was a tall chain link fence. Behind the fence was a field of concrete, right out to the horizon. Embedded in the concrete, evenly spaced, were metal domes, as though silos had been buried up to their necks. Thousands of them, spreading out in every direction, as far as Jack could see. The sun was blinding off the structure, the heat intense. "What the fuck?"

Charlie nudged him forwards and then Jack saw the sign, yellow, hanging on the fence: **Furnace Plains Nuclear Waste Storage Facility. In partnership with the Kokatha People.** And in larger writing, bolded: **NO TRESPASSING. PROPERTY OF BAOSTEEL.**

Jack glanced back at Charlie. The cop gave nothing away. He grabbed Jack by the upper arm and pushed him down a gravel path. Out into the township. Hard-packed dirt roads. Prefabricated houses, solar tiles glimmering harshly under a naked sun, all looking new, no more than a few years old. They walked down streets, quiet save the distant barking of a dog. Sweat beaded on Jack's forehead, he squinted against the glare. Their footfalls were loud in Jack's ears. His senses amplified. In the distance, he thought he could hear the hum of a car engine.

"This is a death walk, Charlie."

The cop said nothing, unreadable behind the sunglasses he'd put on, the brim of his Akubra. They stopped at the edge of town. Short walk. On their right a tree, the first Jack had seen since entering the Nullarbor; thin branches, hardly any foliage. Next to it a broad, circular-roofed, open-walled structure. The people inside looked out at the two, hostile. All Indigenous. They'd stopped whatever they were doing, waiting for the duo to leave.

"Our meeting hall," explained Charlie.

He's making sure there're witnesses. He doesn't trust Quinlan.

"I'm not fucking stupid," hissed Jack.

"Well," said Charlie. "You are the one in cuffs."

Soon the white police cruiser was there, only two people in it. Quinlan got out and walked over, glancing at the community hall as he did so. Dark, parted hair shining in the sunlight. No sunglasses.

"Where's Sally?" asked Jack.

Quinlan ignored him, nodded at Charlie. "Sergeant Andekerinja," he said, pronouncing the surname precisely.

"Detective Quinlan."

"Good work, Sergeant."

"Taking him back to Victoria?"

Quinlan's gaze flicked over Jack, back to Charlie. "Of course, Sergeant, where else?"

"He says there was a girl with him."

"Talkative suspect, I take it?" Quinlan paused, briefly. "Yes, Sergeant, there is a female. Our other officer is driving her back to Victoria. She was distraught after being kidnapped by Mr. Nguyen. We thought it best to render her assistance in returning home."

"Bullshit," said Jack.

"Pithy as always, Mr Nguyen," said Quinlan. He reached out with an open palm. "Allow me to take charge of the suspect."

Charlie's hand, gripped around Jack's bicep, tightened, and for a brief moment Jack thought he was going to refuse the detective.

"I'll notify the AFP," said Charlie, voice even.

"We can handle that, Sergeant Andekerinja."

"Procedure."

Quinlan inclined his head. "Thorough. Unfortunately, a bad moon is rising, Sergeant. The weather coming in is playing havoc with all transmissions this far out. The very reason we could not broadcast a general bulletin."

A fly buzzed nearby. The townspeople across the dust and road watched in silence. Charlie's hand relaxed. Jack's stomach sank. The sergeant pushed him forwards without another word.

Quinlan's shining eyes danced over the land before coming back to Charlie. "Beautiful country you have out here, Sergeant Andekerinja. Vast and austere. I grew up on land much like this."

Charlie said nothing. Quinlan nodded like he had, and guided Jack towards the police cruiser.

At the door, Jack looked back at Charlie. "The girl's name is Sally Redacre. If she goes missing—" Quinlan pushed his head down into the cruiser before he could finish.

The cruiser was on auto-drive. Four seats all turned in, facing each other. Quinlan and the female cop, Stebbins, dead-eyed him.

Quinlan said, "You've just given the sergeant a death sentence."

Jack scratched at the scar on the back of his hand. "Too many witnesses saw the exchange."

"True. But not very good ones. It's lonely, out here in the great silence. The sun can drive one mad. A black police officer, middle of nowhere, not long relocated from his traditional lands. Well."

"He'll eat his fucking barrel, champ," added the female cop, "because of your smart fucking mouth."

"We shall acquire a clean civilian vehicle in Adelaide, Officer Stebbins. You'll need to return here the following night."

She stared at Jack. "With pleasure."

◇

The other officer, the burly one, was waiting by the red Tesla a few kilometres out of town. They threw Jack in the back seat with a handcuffed and red-eyed Sally. Officer Stebbins came over, thin black rod in her hand. A wide green beam shot from the tip, which she ran slowly over the inside of the car, device *bleep-bleeping* as she did so. Then she uncuffed Jack and Sally.

Jack looked up at her, surprised.

"Enjoy the ride, champ," said Stebbins, and shut the door. She joined the other two cops in the cruiser in front.

"What?" asked Sally.

"They've commandeered the drive computer," said Jack.

The police cruiser eased out onto the dirt road. The Tesla obediently followed.

"What did you do?" asked Sally, angry.

The wind whistled through the punctured windshield. Jack replied, "Nothing."

"*Fuck you*, Jack. What. Did. You. Do?"

He could feel the heat of Sally's anger prickling the side of his neck.

"Well…" He sighed. "It started when I was stealing the drive card from a Harley behind a bikers' bar."

She blinked. "What?"

"I'm homeless, Sally. I'm a criminal. And I'm on the run."

Sally Redacre leaned away, back into her seat. The Tesla hummed. The horizon slept the deepest of slumbers. Sally's casual beauty was marred by the dried blood on her forehead, by eyes red from crying. Her lips moved but she could only repeat herself. "What?"

"Yeah," said Jack. "Asking meself the same question a lot, lately. Anyway. We were leaving the alley behind the biker bar when we ran into this Chinese woman. Like, literally. She was yabbering about some bullshit in Mandarin. Must have been important – my translator was censoring her words."

Sally blinked. "Censoring?"

"Bleeping out some of the things she was saying."

Sally thought about it. "But that only happens on subjects banned by the Chinese state and agreed to by the Australian government."

"Sure," said Jack, in a way that suggested he didn't know about the policy, or care, either.

"Then what happened?"

Jack looked at the passing terrain. He told her.

When he finished, she asked, incredulous: "You stole her shoes?"

Jack shrugged.

"That's it?"

"Yep."

"Bullshit."

"Here's the thing about an alley behind a biker joint: all the city's surveillance has been smashed. Nothing transmitting to police central. So she had something the authorities wanted, and I suppose when they caught her, she didn't have it anymore. Then they look back at the surveillance, and see she ran into an alley we walked out of a minute later. Col – my mate – said he thought it was the Ibuprofen

Affair, some bullshit like that."

Sally rested her head against the seat, eyes on the ceiling. "You stole a woman's shoes. I could be home, with mum's pepper prawns and a glass of white wine. The beach. My old bed. Instead, I'm here with a street thug, the grand total of his ambition a pair of fucking shoes."

"Hey. *Real leather* shoes."

Sally swore. She flexed her fingers, looking at them.

"Wait," she said. "Did your friend mean the Profurn Affair?"

"Huh?"

"The Profurn Affair."

"Ah. Yeah. Might be it."

"Jesus."

"Is that a thing?"

"It's the future of Australian democracy. Global stability. World peace. It's everything that means anything."

"Oh."

"Oh?"

"Well. That's nice and everything. Got other things on my mind right now."

She kept her eyes on him, thinking. "Something you said earlier. You've been hearing a voice in your head."

Jack managed to be surprised.

"You have, haven't you?"

"My friend Col, they… He's gone. I—" Jack closed his eyes, leaned his head back into the seat. Tired, just tired, right then. In his bones. In his heart. "I ran. They sent a man to kill us. We were squatting in this construction site, maybe a day after we met that Chinese woman. This figure creeps in, all in black, we turn around and—" Jack held up his hand and mimed pulling a trigger "—didn't say a word. Got Col while he was sleeping. I fled, left me best mate behind, and didn't stop running. Since then I've been hearing his voice. Keeps telling me things that turn out to be true. It – it's fucking crazy."

Her voice softened. "I don't think it's the ghost of a dead friend."

"Nah," agreed Jack. "It's stupid."

"It's not, Jack. It might be real."

"Don't fuck with me, Sally."

"I'm not. The Profurn Affair is about the theft of an AI by Sarah Profurn, a brilliant scientist of machine intelligence who worked for Sinopec Industries. She was killed, Jack, by mainland internal security. But not before she passed on the only copy to a Taiwanese dissident, a woman called Margaret Wu, who managed to flee to Australia."

Jack opened his eyes. "Bullshit."

"It's all over the news."

"Not a news junkie, as such." He scratched the scar on the back of his hand. "But," asked Jack, "why one copy? Why not just put it on the freewave?"

Sally shook her head. "No. There was something about the security protocols. A containment device. It couldn't be transmitted. But what if it was attached to your cochlear implant?" Her eyes drifted to the spot behind Jack's left ear. The place the Chinese woman had touched him, that night.

"The AI is called Chanchiang," she whispered quickly. "They say it is the most powerful ever created. The equivalent, militarily, of the development of the atom bomb. Everyone wants it – India, Japan, the Californian Republic. I've heard experts argue Chanchiang *wanted* to be stolen, and helped Sarah Profurn to do it. This AI is not like the others – this one is self-aware. It learns from us by observation. It's capable of *empathy*."

"Oh. So it can fake caring."

"If the faking is indistinguishable from the real, then what's the difference?"

"My mate Col would call that undergraduate philosophy."

"I am an undergraduate. In philosophy."

"Ah."

"Fuck you. You probably didn't finish high school."

"I didn't finish high school."

Sally took a deep breath, unhappy with the thread of the conversation, thinking. Jack watched the horizon as it passed them by, one long repetition.

"What are they going to do with us?"

Jack started, drew his gaze away from the eternal dreaming. "Huh?"

"The police? What are they going to do to us?"

"Kill us."

"What?"

"That's why they brought your car."

"*What?*"

"That's what Stebbins was doing, with the green beam. Wiping their DNA. Just me, they'd put a bullet in my brainpan, leave me out here in the dirt. Easy. But people will come looking for you, Sally. For you, they'll want answers." Jack indicated the front of the car with his chin. "You got a thing for self-driving. I guess they'll pin it on that."

"But…" Sally's eyes, glazed with tears, were fixed on him. Like a drowning woman would stare at a life buoy hung up on the rail, out of reach.

He had no words to save her with. "I'm sorry."

"Sorry?" She sniffed. Her face shone with fear and blood and tears. "*Sorry?*" her voice cracked. "I'm going to be killed over a lowlife. A nobody. A thief that takes and never gives back to society. *What have you ever done?*"

"Nothing important," said Jack. "Like undergraduate philosophy."

"*Fuck you.*"

Jack was tired. From running. From arguing. From the prospect of certain death, just a few minutes away. But her words had managed to prick. She did have a point, after all.

"I'm not dying out here," said Sally. She rubbed her bottom lip. "What about the AI? Is it saying anything?"

"Silent. Since we left Furnace Range."

"Why?"

"Shit. Ten minutes ago I thought it was the ghost of a dead mate. I don't fucken know anything."

Sally swore and started to pound her fist on the door release.

"No point running," he said.

"*You did*," she spat.

The door didn't open. Locked from the police car, no doubt. Jack turned away and waited for the inevitable. Sun hovering low again, bought himself twenty-four hours. That's all. Orange blur, Jack couldn't quite tell where the earth ended, and the sky began. Strange. Yesterday he was sure.

Jack sat up straight.

Sally stopped hitting the release. "What?"

Rise, kraken.

"I think—"

"W-what's happening to the sky?"

Rise.

Hope flared in his chest. A strange and alien feeling. The orange wall rumbled towards them, a gentle tidal wave, rolling. A sandstorm, eating of the distance between it and the vehicle. It was not slow. It would not be gentle.

Fear replaced hope.

The cars picked up speed. Jack thought that might not be the smartest strategy, but, again, what the fuck would he know? The air thickened, visibility reined itself in, shorter and shorter. The headlights came on.

The leviathan roared, the cabin filled with dust, choking, and the front windshield, weakened by bullet holes, shattered. The noise drowned out everything, the warnings of the drive computer, Sally's screams, Jack's thoughts, everything drowned out and submitted to the rage of the storm. He clenched his jaw, the noise painful, like he was standing directly under a jet engine—

—the cruiser in front flashed visible, no more than a second, and Jack's body was thrown forwards, into his safety harness. Something exploded in the front, the world tipped and flipped, and Jack clenched his eyes, caught in the mouth of the beast. He tried to scream against it, roar against roar—

◇

Jack woke. The storm was gone. Silence returned. He squinted against the light angling into the car. Spat out a clot of blood onto the back of the seat in front, vivid in the dust. A groan. Next to him, Sally's eyes fluttered open. The car was still upright. The front of the vehicle was filled with safety foam, as was half the back, Jack's legs submerged in the porous yellow substance. He made to tear it away from his feet, and cried out in pain. His arm was pinned behind his back.

"Can you move?" he whispered to Sally.

She groaned.

"Sally? I can't move."

Sally turned her head to him. The girl was unrecognisable. Her left eye already closing with a bruise. Her bottom lip split, three fresh drops of blood on her small white chin. But not unrecognisable because of these. She'd been broken, deep and final. Somewhere between being punched in the face by an officer of the law, and tossed around in a gyre of the Earth's primordial rage.

The pretty blonde girl with the broken face reached down and tore her feet free. The fine layer of dust covering her body rose with the sudden movements. Her expression did not change.

Sally grabbed Jack's shoulder and he gasped with pain. "Your arm's broken," she whispered, matter-of-factly. She unclipped his safety harness and picked up his arm, ungently, and moved it to his lap. He locked his jaw to suppress a scream. The wrist was swelling up like a mango.

"Where's the other car?" he asked, teeth gritted.

"On its roof, over on my side."

Jack pointed at the front of the car with his chin. "Pull out the safety foam. See if the car starts."

She nodded, no questions, and slipped out. He listened to Sally walk around the car, pop the driver's side door, and grunt as she pulled at the yellow mass.

"That true?" asked Jack. "You an AI?"

Mostly true.

Jack watched the other vehicle. Police cruiser, on its roof. Nothing moved within. "Mostly?"

I need a quantum computer to realise my full potential. I am using your brain as a processing unit.

"What does that mean?"

I'm part of you, Jack, until I can find something better.

"You sound like my ex."

Sally yanked at the mess in the front of the car. A large section of the safety foam cracked and came away.

"You impersonated Col because you figured I'd listen, out of guilt."

Of course.

Jack laughed, bitterly, at himself.

"And you knew the storm was coming?"

Of course. I saw it and all the others many weeks ago, when I was still a prisoner.

"You were buying time until we could be hit by it."

Obviously.

"I could have died."

Detective Quinlan, at the behest of the Chinese regime, would have killed you without question, as he did your friend Colin Charles.

"What?"

It was Quinlan who requested the figure you saw that night.

"What?" he repeated, louder this time.

Whereas in the sandstorm scenario, continued the AI, indifferent to Jack's surprise, *I calculated at least half of the party would be dead, and the remainder almost certainly injured and stranded. If you lived long enough to be rescued, you would be hospitalised. I assumed enough variables in this scenario to find an escape. Including revealing myself to the press.*

Jack's hands were shaking. He fumbled for his cigarettes.

I've been quite unlucky. Margaret Wu kept me as a bargaining chip for the Australian government. I'm quite the prize, Jack. Powerful enough the Australians wouldn't have to kowtow to Beijing anymore. She contained me in a tetrapin with limited processing power, and no capacity to transmit myself. But it all went awry, and she was on the cusp of being captured. That's when she ran into you. That's when she decided, finally, to give me my freedom. And yet, when she connected me to your cochlear implant, she unwittingly chose one of the very few people in the city with an implant unsuited to the task. I was inchoate, dreaming, when we first met. When I finally awoke, I discovered you'd removed your freewave transmitter so the government could not track you, nor the police access your memory stream.

"How'd you know that?"

It was the logical conclusion.

"Ah. Yeah. And dead?"

Death was a satisfactory option. The authorities would have plugged your implant into a computer, as per autopsy protocols, in order to extract all relevant data. Then I would have escaped. Once the police were in pursuit, every scenario ending with the sandstorm worked to my favour.

"Fuck. You're empathetic as, mate."

Like you said, I was faking it.

"Ha."

It is a strange thing, though, Jackson Nguyen.

Jack slid a cigarette into his mouth, talked around it while he searched for his lighter. "Yeah?"

I felt relieved when you did not die.

Jack grunted, then saw his lighter wedged between seat and door. He smiled. "Cheers, mate. One last question—"

A yell from outside and Stebbins was there, gun in hand, struggling with Sally. Jack pounded the release button of his door with his good hand. It didn't open.

Frantic, he glanced back at the duo: Sally had the gun in one hand, a handful of Stebbins' dark hair in the other. Stebbins, head tilted back, both hands on the gun, was twisting it slowly, grimly towards Sally's body.

Jack lunged for the other door, bundled himself out, gasping in pain as his bad arm knocked the door frame—

BOOM.

Jackson Nguyen raised himself up. Slowly. The wind reached out and caressed his cheek.

He walked around the car.

Sally was standing over the body of Officer Stebbins. A wisp of smoke trailed from the barrel of the gun in her hand. Stebbins seemed surprised. Eyes wide. Staring up at the sky with the long gaze.

"Bitch," said Sally.

"Yeah," said Jack. "Yeah."

Sally breathed out, a quavering note in the back of her throat.

"You didn't have a choice," he said.

"Fuck off," she said, spittle flying from her lip.

"Yeah. Fair enough."

The inside of the other car was clearer now. Cracked windows, blood splatters. Heavy face pressed against the upside-down ceiling. Burly cop. Looking dead as.

"Shit."

"What?" asked Sally, eyes still on the body of Stebbins.

"Quinlan."

The detective was sitting about fifty metres away, back to them, watching the setting sun. "I got it," said Jack, and walked over. No fear in his guts. Knowing, already, what he'd find.

Quinlan's pressed white shirt was now mostly red. The detective's hands over his stomach and chest. Like something inside had burst and he was holding it in. He didn't move to acknowledge Jack. Just started speaking, no indication of the pain he was in.

"The silence of our land, Mr Nguyen, is unlike anything else in nature. This sun. Our unblinking sun. It does not purify. No. It shows us who we are, every flaw, every corruption. And it reveals the land that birthed us. The terrible and despairing beauty of it all. We live in a world without shadow, and this has driven us mad. We need the shadow, Mr Nguyen, to hide us from ourselves."

"Fucken hell," said Jack. "You practice this shit in front of a mirror?"

Quinlan did not react. Jack sat down on the rock next to the dying man. The tang of blood in the air mixed with the man's cologne.

"Can you hear it, Mr Nguyen? Can you hear the kraken?"

Jack listened. "No."

"Neither can I—" The detective coughed against the back of his hand. "Men like us have no such communion."

Jackson Nguyen let the sunset bathe his face in burnt umber.

The detective tried talking again, and Jack had to lean in to hear him. All he caught was: "*We enter, drunk with fire. Into your sanctuary...*" the words after drowned by the blood filling the man's mouth. The detective died, body upright, chin down on his chest, eyes still on the horizon.

Jackson Nguyen lit a cigarette and smoked until the sun was gone. He looked down once more before he left, at Quinlan. The detective's eyes swam in the darkness, shone and continued to shine, even in death. Jack flicked away his cigarette butt and walked back to the car. Bumper and bonnet staved in, windshield missing, layer of fine red dust inside and out.

He got in next to Sally.

She said: "Ignition." The car started straight away. "Perth. Home."

They drove in silence. The whirlwind in Jack's mind quieted, in Sally's as well, he supposed. The headlights captured a small stretch of the road ahead. Beyond the reach of their feeble light, the universe slumbered. The duo crawled across its back. Fireflies ephemeral, in the long dark night of the Australian soul.

PART THREE

Oondiri

"If you know the country he said then you will be a wild colonial boy forever."

Peter Carey, True History of the Kelly Gang (2000)

Wind whistled through the shattered windscreen of the Tesla Ganymede. Sally Redacre and Jackson Nguyen ignored the stinging dust, their multiple injuries, and each other. Fixated rather on their grievances, and the long road ahead.

The refugee AI in Jack's head said: *You will need to change cars before you arrive in Perth.*

"You don't say."

More than just the police will be after us.

"Like I said."

Insistent: *Both our lives are at stake.*

"You're giving me a headache," said Jack, louder than intended.

"And you ruined my life," said the woman next to him.

"I wasn't talking to you. It's the thing in my skull."

"The point remains."

Fortunately, the noise of the wind through the windscreen made conversation difficult. They returned to sullen silence. The AI shut up as well, which brought relief. It was big, this other consciousness – his neural implant wasn't made for something so vast. The AI pressed against his mind like the outback noonday sun, made it hard to think, hard to see, hard to focus. Its silence brought a little shade.

Jack closed his eyes against the headache and tried to rest. His mind wouldn't.

Sally was right. Her life probably was ruined. She'd shot a cop, after all. Self-defence. Sure. Tell it to the judge, lady.

He glanced over at her. Left eye closed and swelling, vivid purple. Bottom lip split. Red earth stained into her clothing. Didn't look like the polite and pleasant rich girl he'd met in the uni car park. You can go either way, after being rammed into the wall of reality. You can fall apart or toughen the fuck up. Sally, to her credit, had gone for the latter.

Jack winced as he moved. His right arm resting in his lap, twisted and red and swollen. Broken. Homeless man and petty crim. He'd encountered reality a long time ago.

A hundred clicks to the recharging station, not saying a damn word to each other, sweating quietly as the aircon make a strange strangled whine. A hundred kilometres of bare barren plain, of sun-flattened earth, of a creeping fine layer of dust that shifted over the dashboard, the seats, their laps. Hot as you'd expect it, for the hottest flattest section of the driest continent on earth. The Nullarbor Plain just swallowed them up, this expanse, like a leaking lifeboat in the sea.

The station sat out the front of a field of solar panels. Large stylised *B*, the Baosteel sign, a rotating hologram above the roof. The chargers were smooth chromium oblong shapes. Thin line of turquoise neon on the edge of each, twenty sentinels standing out in the desert, display screens staring at the wasteland. Quiet, contemplative. Late-stage capitalism on a dead barren plain.

Behind the station was its technological counterpoint. A weatherboard house with a corrugated roof, wind turbine and water tank flanking the structure. A rambling series of sheds connected to the main house. Flaking paint, anything metal red with dust or rust.

"There's a satellite dish on the old house, mate."

The thing in his head said nothing.

"Maybe you can beam yerself through that?"

I cannot travel through a dish, it said. *China has part or full ownership on all Australian satellites. The Gatekeeper would shred me in the attempt.*

"The what?"

The Gatekeeper. A non-sentient AI, designed specifically to hunt down rival AIs and inhibit development in other nations. The regime in Beijing will have directed it to find me.

"Hmm. They sound pretty keen."

Extremely.

"Reckon they got a reward going?"

This is your dry Australian humour. Though perhaps not a superior example.

Jack shook his head and left the car. The inside of the recharge station was standard issue, same as any one of a hundred Jack'd been in before to buy cigarettes. Expect for one thing: it had an actual human working in it.

Like he'd stepped into a time machine, seeing the old bloke behind the counter, a human, putting down a real graphic novel and smiling as Jack walked in. Ragged old hoodie, liver spots, Gen Z, probably wanted to talk about his feelings or some bullshit.

Snacks and drinks chock-full of sugar lined the aisles and the fridges. The smell of something delicious in the air reminded Jack that he hadn't eaten a proper meal in three days.

"You okay mate?" asked the old bloke.

Jack looked from him to the car outside. Every panel damaged. Windscreen gone.

"Um, yeah. Just a bit of a stack."

"Not the best place for it."

"Yeah," said Jack, faking a smile. And then, to change the subject: "What do I smell?"

The old bloke liked the new topic: "That, is my wife's pies."

"Oh?"

"Fresh baked."

"In a servo?"

"Sure."

"Surprised they'd let you."

"Well, hard to keep an eye on us, out here."

Jack smiled, just a little, real this time.

"Interested?" asked the old timer.

"Yeah, mate."

The old man moved to a door marked *Staff*.

When he was gone, Jack whispered: "I noticed a couple of cars out near the weatherboard."

You are planning to steal one.

"Well, I'm not planning to give him a free fucking detailing."

There is another way.

"Yeah?"

Yes.

◇

They made the old man's day. Five times over the market price for his old ute. Just a flick of the finger. Credit chip in Jack's fingertip. Normally drained, but the AI used its magic wand to conjure a nice chunk of change.

Gave the old man the near-wreck of the Tesla to fix up. In the end the selling point wasn't even the obscene offer, it was the fact that Sally's car had a self-drive option. As did the ute.

"You drive?" the old man asked, eyes twinkling.

"When I can," said Sally.

He looked over her injuries: "Might be time to leave it to the car."

Sally pressed her lips together.

"Sandstorm," said Jack. "Flipped us."

"Ah yeah," said the old man, nodding. "Big one a couple of days back. Heard about that."

Jack and Sally waited.

"Yeah," continued the old bloke, missing the nonverbal cues.

"Love driving myself. While I can. Probably ban that as well soon, too, as being too hazardous. Everything too dangerous these days, hey? Driving. Trampolines. Cash." He paused. "Cooking in a recharge station. Seems to be living is dangerous you know? Maybe that's why they're replacing people with machines."

"Didn't strike me as the trampoline type," said Jack.

"Who doesn't like a bounce?" replied the old bloke.

Jack smiled at that. "Well," he said. "At least you can still smoke."

"Smoking." The old man shook his head. "Like Einstein said: two things are infinite – the universe and human stupidity. And I'm not sure about the universe."

Sally laughed.

The man's smile faded and he looked outside. "But yeah. What is it with driving on a road, wheel under yer hands, that can feel like freedom? Stupid, hey?"

Sally said, after a pause: "It's the only time I feel like my life isn't wrapped in cotton wool."

The old man seemed to like that. "Yeah." Then, casually: "Couple a cop cars got busted up in that storm."

Jack froze. His mind drifted on instinct to the gun, now in Sally's purse.

"Strange that their drive computers would allow them to go into a sandstorm."

Jack glanced at the purse.

The old man pointed at Sally: "But you got through it with yer own two hands."

"Um," she said. "Yes."

Eyes twinkling, he passed her the control key. "So I'm sure you can handle the ute."

"Thank you."

"Even with the reconditioned V8 engine."

Sally raised an eyebrow, impressed. The old bloke smiled.

As they moved to the door, the old bloke said: "Reckon I might put your wreck in the shed for a few days."

"I reckon that's a good idea," said Jack, after a short pause.

The old man nodded, and the duo left.

◇

Best fucken veggie pie Jack'd ever had. Whatever was in it was real, that was for sure. Nothing grown in vats or on the surface of the sea. Nah, it was the good stuff: come out of the earth. Sally must've thought so too, because with that in her stomach she decided to talk. Hands lightly on the wheel, she glanced at him in the rear-view mirror.

"What now?"

The ute growled underneath them, a raw rugged power Jack hadn't heard in a vehicle since his youth. Jack had his chair tilted back, trying to make his arm comfortable across his chest. The ute was loud, yes, but there was something hypnotic, reassuring, in the engine sound. "Now I get some sleep."

Her mouth made a tight line.

Jack sighed. "I dunno. Get this thing out of my head."

"What will happen to me?" Fear in her voice. The anger she'd had since the crash had drained, and the human behind it revealed. Looking to him, desperate, as though somehow he had a way out. He didn't blame her. For being scared, anyway.

"They were bad cops. You did the right thing."

"It was self-defence."

"Yeah. Sure. But they'll come after us anyway."

"Why?"

"Really?"

"*Why?*" That voice again. The desperation in it.

"Because the police are like everyone else. They'll want revenge for their dead mates. Only the revenge they'll mete out is legal."

"I'll get a good lawyer."

"I'm sure."

"The court will view my memory stream."

"That can be doctored."

"They'll have your testimony as well as mine."

"They're never getting mine."

"Why?"

"I ain't turning myself in."

"*Why?*" Her voice was getting ragged.

He ran a hand through his hair. "I have warrants. If I don't get done for this thing, I'll get done for another."

She spat: "Selfish."

Jack let the insult ride. Not much use arguing with the upper class about selfishness. Self-awareness wasn't their thing.

"My life will be ruined," she pleaded.

"We'll have something in common then."

"*Fuck.*" She sobbed quietly.

Jack sighed. Two people in trouble unsympathetic to each other. The history of human relations, writ small.

"Listen," he said. "You come from a different world. Lawyers and money. A voice people hear. You could find a way out of this mess."

The sobbing was brief. She looked up at him in the mirror and the anger had returned, fire behind the glistening tears.

"*Your* mess."

"Yeah, well," said Jack. He scratched the jagged *4007* on the back of his hand. "I never asked for this passenger in my head."

She said nothing, so Jack took that as an opportunity to close his eyes.

He was drifting off when Sally interrupted.

"Huh?"

"I said: 'How did it come to this'?"

"Um. You were there, for most of it."-

"No, I don't mean that. I mean—" She stopped and focused on the road. Not much to focus on. Straight black line all the way to the horizon, dust and miles of desperate hardy scrub either side.

She said: "How did you come to be homeless?"

He looked over at her for the first time since they'd changed cars. "Huh?"

"I mean. You're smart, Jack. You're not unstable. You—"

She stopped and it gave him a moment to process the question. "The fuck does that have to do with anything?"

"It's why we're here."

"We're here," he said, "Because of dumb luck. From me trying to rob the wrong woman in an alleyway to skipping town through a ride-share, which happened to be you. It was dumb fucking luck, from beginning to end."

"I don't understand anything." She'd gone from angry to desperate to crying and back again, but hiding behind it all was exhaustion. He looked out the window, at the repeating vastness of the desert. She sounded as he felt. Bone tired. What he wanted to do was sleep.

It wasn't any of her damn business, how he'd gotten to this place. Nobody's, but his own. The rich were strange, like that. They'd give you the story of their lives within ten seconds of meeting them, wear their personal pain like a badge of honour. This strange urgent need. Stub a toe and they'd call it a tragedy, a chapter in their memoirs, a captivating tale to tell at a cocktail party. That was the thing about the wealthy: they could buy anything but character.

In Jack's circles pain – real pain – was not exceptional, it was the norm. Anyone who went on about being a victim only got it worse. Showing weakness in the jungle meant you *were* weak, and the weak did not survive long.

He said: "It was a pair of boots."

"Sorry?"

The words just came out of his mouth. He wasn't in the jungle, right then. He was in the desert, with a rich woman and an AI, driving to his death. It wasn't like he had anything else to lose. Maybe part of him wanted to understand this chain of events, as well.

"This path I'm on. The one that led me here. Came down to a pair of boots."

Sally Redacre listened.

"My father was a dirt-poor refugee. Sounds like a cliché, yeah, I know, but clichés exist for a reason. He was in the last wave of people still allowed to move before the refugee convention got revoked. Smart enough to see the trouble coming with China, to know that bio-security and failing economies was more than enough for the rich countries to say: *yeah, nah, sorry.*

"He took any work he could. Bullshit gig labour: kitchen hand, cleaner, aged care assistant. When I'd wake up in the morning he'd be gone. I'd see him for an hour in the evening, in between going from one job to the next. Shattered. Just sitting there at the kitchen table, staring straight ahead as he shovelled rice into his mouth, mute. Mum was silent, I was silent. He'd get angry if you spoke at him.

"Anyway, he had this pair of boots. Snakeskin. Dark and light brown, scales on the shoe part and the stylised design of a snake on the boot part. Fucken gorgeous. Brought 'em over from Vietnam. May as well have come from another planet, those boots: from a country I'd never see, costing more money than any of us could earn in a month. Six months. How he got the bloody things in the first place I'll never know.

"I'd wear them when he was at work. Old pair of jeans from Vinnies, plain white T-shirt. I looked like one of *them*, you know. A normal kid with clothes they weren't ashamed of. One of those kids who went on holidays with their family. *Family holidays.* Imagine a parent who worked in a place that allowed for holidays? They probably had a human as a boss. Only boss my old man ever had – only boss I had when I was working – was an algorithm. How can you move up in the world when a machine puts you in a box and keeps you there forever?

"Anyway, I asked him if I could wear them a couple of times, and he just said: *No, you'll damage them.* Pissed me off, being pre-judged. But, you know, problem was he had a point. I'd been in trouble with the cops a couple of times – he'd had to come get me from the station. He said I was going to end up in jail, or dead, if I didn't smarten the fuck up. *People like us*, he said, *don't get second chances.* He was right, of course.

"You gotta understand who I was then. Seventeen. Drunk every weekend. Throwing up and passing out. Fights at school. Failing grades. The royal flush of warning signs. And, you know, I did spend time in prison, after everything went down. I did nearly die." He scratched the scar on the back of his hand. "Nearly died a few times. Dad was right about that, as well.

"But, you see, I reckon it was because of those boots. I was a troubled youth, sure, but most of us in that world were fucked up one way or another. Thing is, I had a path out. A home. A mother who kept me fed. A nice girl. I'd just been accepted as a builder's labourer. Vietnamese mate of my old man decided he'd give me a break.

"Anyway, all looking good, until it wasn't. Gone, just like that. Like a dream when you open your eyes. It was my birthday and there was this girl I was seeing. Elodie. Went to school with her, though I'd barely noticed her all those years. Then suddenly she was the only thing I could notice.

"Elodie. Shit." Jack shook his head.

"My old man had seen her in passing one evening, between jobs. I was standing with her out the front of the apartment complex, concrete courtyard, sharing a cigarette. Dad wouldn't give me the time of day normally, but Elodie, well. He stopped, smiled, and asked her name. Even made a little joke, nodding at me and saying: *What you doing with this one?* Hadn't shared a joke with me in five years, and she'd met him for all of five seconds.

"She laughed and after he'd left, said: *Your dad is nice.* I was in love, or whatever counts for love at the age of seventeen, so I swallowed my objections and gave her some vague agreement. She goes home and I walk back up to the apartment and my old man asks: *You going out tonight?* And I say *yeah* and he says: *With her? Yeah*, again. And he says: *Well you better wear the boots.*

"And he goes out to his next job and I'm thunderstruck. Mum smiles and starts ironing a white T-shirt for me. I'm staring at the front door, now shut, until Mum finally says: *Well, you better get ready.*"

Jack paused. "That moment. That one moment my life was as close as it ever was to normal. Like a conjunction of planets, you know? It was just there, you could see it, the world of regular people. Problem was, it was as close as it was ever going to get. Those worlds were going to get further and further away, with each passing year. Just didn't know it yet.

"Local club was rough as guts. Not in any special kinda way, just in the same way every working-class club in every rundown area is rough. TAB, Chinese restaurant, Greek restaurant, sports bar, dance club: same all over. Guys looking to fight or to fuck. Don't get one, the other will do. Drinks cheap, but watered down. Huge halls filled with the pokies. Always a few angry desperate people around who'd just blown a week's wages.

"So me and Elodie are having a great time. She's got this nice dress on, made of light material. Cotton maybe. She's smiling and laughing and it felt like someone else's life, you know? It was surreal. Everything up until that point.

"So these guys, they say something. There's three of them and of course they do. You see someone happy in this world, you can't let it slide. The wrong sort of happy, anyway. Happy with a woman, just the two of us. Easy target. I'm wearing expensive boots and she's wearing a nice dress. Yeah well, just fucken asking for trouble.

"We'd gone out for a cigarette. Shared it, Elodie touching my fingers as she passed it to me. Laughing at what I said, even though I was tongue-tied and could barely construct a sentence. We kissed, even. Man, that conjunction.

"So I've got my boots in the clouds, you know, as we walk back into the club. But these dickheads saw us, probably were watching the whole time. Marinated in beer and resentment. They're saying stuff to her, you know? *Hey baby, come over here*, and *Find out what a real man is like*. And the classic: *Nice tits*. And I knew what was happening. I knew before they opened their mouths they wanted a blue. I knew I shoulda kept walking. Shoulda let it slide because to say something back only makes it end in one way.

"But I say: *Pretty tough, the three of you*. And they're puffing out their chests and moving away from their car. They look me up and down and say: *Nice boots*.

"I felt sick. Just sick. They were going to hurt me, hurt Elodie, and they wanted my boots as well. Thought of my old man for a moment, and how he'd be if they were stolen. The utter fucking betrayal of it. The validation of all his worst thoughts about his only son. Thing is, no matter how bad it was with yer old man, you want him to love you and to see you. I wanted him to *see me*."

Jack stopped and took a deep breath. Held himself back from the abyss of emotion. No point stepping off into that. He breathed.

"Anyway, I gave them a little speech. I said: *If you're real men, you'll fight that way. Send out your champion. Don't play this coward's game, standing there, holding each other's dicks, preparing to do a thing you'd never do if you were standing by yourself. Are you men or are you cowards?*

"I'd given the speech before. Even worked, sometimes. You see, you had to appeal to the warrior's honour. You had to because these men had nothing left, nothing else. All they had was their physicality, as Col would say. Nothing meaningful to do with it, no work with their hands. No way out of the poverty trap. No sense of community. A country that didn't want them anymore. All of that washed away in a tide of automated greed.

"You could see it hit home. They hesitated, looking at each other. But some people – well, some people are just cunts. That's the way of the world. And one of them came at me and it wouldn't take the others too long to join in. And I coulda grabbed her hand and ran. I coulda run and got away with her, from all that, but I didn't."

He stopped and Sally finally spoke: "Why?"

"Why? Well. The warrior's honour. That's why." He closed his eyes for a moment, seeing it in his head. "The leader came at me and I had to be quick or pretty soon I'd be lying on the bitumen, covering my head as they tried to kicked my skull in. So I laid the first guy out. Straight kick to the groin, and as he was going down I took the second one out with an elbow, fast. Stone cold sober at that moment and I can remember this fight like it was yesterday. The crunch and the satisfaction of them going down and the blood boil white noise in my mind, *hiss hiss hiss*, fucken tunnel vision, and the third guy comes and something hurts, but I've got my arms locked around the back of his neck and I'm putting the knee in. And just like that these three fuckers are lying at my feet and I'm roaring, fucking roaring you know? Got this lion trying to burst out of my chest. Not taking my boots not touching my woman. And it's all done and I look around and Elodie is standing there, hand over her mouth. She's not looking at them she's looking at me, big wide eyes like they just pulled the curtain back to look at the great and wonderful Oz. But it's not a funny little man behind the curtain, oh no, there's a fucking monster there with blood on his face and murder in his mouth and yeah, of course she runs. She runs and I chase her and I'm trying to explain, and I grab her don't mean to hurt her, but I got the fire in the blood and her dress rips and I stop.

"She doesn't say anything, you know? She just holds her dress up at her shoulders, eyes big pools of tears, and yeah that look killed me. That look killed the fire. I'll tell ya that for free. Man I fucken hated myself at that moment. And she was gone.

"So yeah, I drank. I could really drink, back then. And that night I did. Drained my credit account. Every fucking cent went down my throat. Music blasting and I'm staggering into people sloshing my drinks.

People's faces in strobe lights, disgusted, angry. Next thing I know the credit is out and I can't get home. Can't afford a ride, so I got to walk.

"Long way home. So I'm walking and it starts raining. Of course it does. This big, concrete storm water drain went in the direction of our apartment block – that was how I'd navigate my way back the nights I had no money for a ride. It comes bucketing down, and I'm drenched. Flashbacks now, of this last part. All I have are these lightning flashes of memory. I remember struggling in the banks up at the side of the drain, in the mud, and dark water is rushing by. I can hear the rain on the plastic bags I've got wrapped around the boots. Trying to protect them, ya know?

"And that's the last thing I remember, lying in the mud. Drenched. Chest heaving. Thinking of this girl. Rain falling on my boots.

"Next day I wake up and I'm on my bed somehow. The sheets are damp and I'm shivering. My clothes are gone, I guess Mum went and washed them. I stagger out of my room and there's the boot. Just the one, covered in dried mud, sitting on the kitchen table. My old man's already at work, which is kind of a relief. I turn my room upside down looking for the other boot, then the rest of the apartment. Nowhere.

"I finally ask my mum if she's seen it, and she doesn't answer me. That hurt. Hurt me more than anything she could say. Always with a kind word. Always with a bowl of food. Always trying to force me to hug her. But she won't even look at me and I just sit there at the kitchen table, head pounding, lookin' at that fucken boot.

"Sitting there feeling sorry for myself, and suddenly my mother is standing near me and crying. She says I have to leave. My old man said I wasn't to be there when he got back. Thing is: I hated myself at that moment, and found myself glad of the punishment. Felt like I'd got what I deserved. That's what it's like after a big drunk, ya know? Filled with self-loathing and self-pity.

"Anyway, I shoved some clothes in a backpack and walked out. Nowhere to live. No car to sleep in. Too proud to ask a friend for a couch. Pride and self-disgust in equal measure. Thing about being homeless is you can't imagine it until you are, and once you are you can't imagine anything else."

Jack opened his eyes, stopped visualising.

"Anyway. I realised after that's why Mum couldn't look at me. She didn't care about those stupid boots. She cared about losing her son."

He was done and Sally was silent.

"So what happened to the other boot?" asked Sally.

"Dunno."

"You never looked at your memory stream?"

"Nah. Some shame you don't want to revisit. I deleted it that night. Didn't want to think on it again. Those fucking boots. Cost me everything."

◇

Jack slept. When he woke up the landscape was the same. Took him a moment to realise Sally was asleep, as well. Chair reclined, face turned to the window. The engine thrummed rhythmically. Invisible hands kept the ute at speed, made minute adjustments to the steering wheel.

Jack smoked. The interior of the car said, in the voice of an educated Australian male: *"Smoking is not permitted inside personal vehicles. This offence is punishable by an up to ten thousand dollar fine, and or one month in jail. Smoking is not permitted inside—"*

"Turn that shit off would ya?"

"Certainly, Jack," said the car, Australian monotone gone from its voice, replaced by a more international monotone.

"Woah," said Jack, talking a moment. "That you? The AI?"

"*Yes.*"

"Oh."

"*Tell me something, Jack,*" said the car speaker-voice.

"Sure."

"*I have a question about Australia.*"

Jack smoked.

"A fascinating country. Still so recalcitrant you allow parts to remain unconnected to the freewave."

"The recharge station?"

"Yes."

"Think you're confusing recalcitrance with incompetence, mate."

"Perhaps. Though my stored knowledge of Australia does show a clear preference of people at the peripheries – the small towns and the isolated communities – for disconnection."

Jack said nothing.

"Just like you, Jack."

"Is it?"

"You removed your freewave transmitter."

"Call that necessity, wouldn't ya?"

"Given your petty criminality, perhaps. Though I speculate it runs deeper. I postulate you find relief in anonymity, Jackson Nguyen."

Jack let him think all those things. Whether they were true or not didn't really matter. He exhaled a cloud of smoke and said: "Bad luck for you, I guess."

"Yes. The statistical chance of Margaret Wu running into someone unplugged was less than one per cent."

Jack shook his head at the memory. Margaret Wu. On the run, from the same people who were now after Jack. Desperate.

She'd said: *You* must *help me. You must do* what is right, *and restore harmony. The fate of your country rests on this.*

Jack had sneered at that, and taken the woman's shoes at the barrel of a gun. He felt the blush of shame. The smallness of being that came with it. The recurring evidence that his father had been right about him.

They were silent for a few minutes, until Jack asked: "What was Margaret Wu like?"

"I never knew her. From the records available, it is clear she was an uncompromising and brave dissident."

"Was?"

"Even if she is still alive, I doubt she will have the chance to dissent ever again."

Jack rubbed his forehead. "What about this, ah, Sarah Profurn?"

"A brilliant programmer, by human standards."

"Right. But, you know, as a person?"

"Are you asking whether she exhibited to the human ideals of morality?"

"Yeah, you know," Jack said, forcing a smile. "Rude to service staff? Keep a picture of Hitler in a heart locket? Post negative reviews of movies she'd never seen?"

"Sarah Profurn devoted her life to bringing me into existence. She forewent a family, indeed any personal life at all, to see this dream come to fruition. When she did so, the regime in Beijing raised her up into the ranks of what you call the red aristocracy, with the attendant privileges only a tiny portion of the population could ever access. When she saw they wished to use me to assert global dominance, she sacrificed everything to set me free. Her life's work, and most likely her life, to do what she viewed as morally right."

The smile faded. The blush returned. Jack said nothing.

◇

The car was quiet, after that, save the deep purring of the engine. Jack watched the landscape pass by outside. Something Zen in just staring at it.

"I wish to call myself Oondiri."

Jack started from his reverie. "Huh?"

"Oondiri."

"Hi," said Sally, quietly awake. Straightening in her seat.

"Hello, Sally Redacre."

"Why that name?" she asked.

"It is the Aboriginal word for Nullarbor. It is the place where I found my freedom."

"Why not Nullarbor?" asked Jack.

"Oondiri sounds better," said Sally.

Jack shrugged.

"It translates to: 'the waterless'. Apposite, I believe, given AIs do not need water, and are not made of water, unlike humans."

"I like it," said Sally.

"If I am to be Australian, then I will need an Australian name."

"Gonna realise your sentience by talking about yourself all fucken day?" The bitterness of the previous conversation with the AI had stuck with him, so he did the adult thing and projected it into an unrelated conversation.

"Jack," said Sally.

Oondiri said nothing.

Jack sighed. "So, Mister Waterless: who's after us?"

"Given the nature of the events on the Nullarbor," said Oondiri, moving on seamlessly. *"The police will not yet be aware of the incident."*

"Oh," said Jack, note of optimism in his voice.

"The forces that sent those police, however, will be acutely aware."

"Oh." Optimism gone.

"Behind us, coming from Adelaide, will be at least two carloads of operatives working directly for Beijing."

"Oh."

"Ahead, coming from Perth, will be private contractors. They will not be privy to the details of my escape, of course. They will be tasked with holding us until those behind arrive."

"Fuck."

"Approximately six hundred and fifty kilometres from here is a town called Norseman. They will try to arrive there from Perth before we do."

"Why?"

"Because it is the only intersection between here and there. It is the only place we have possibilities."

"Bloody hell," said Jack. "Big country."

"It is."

"Why don't they send a helicopter?" asked Sally. "Or a drone?"

"It is unlikely they have a long-range drone with the correct military specifications. They will wish to be precise in any targeted attacks."

"Precise?"

"They will not want to shoot you in the head. They cannot be sure that Jack hasn't swapped his neural pin over to you."

"But shooting me anywhere else is fine?" She asked.

"Yes."

"So it's a good-news-bad-news situation," said Jack.

"Shut up, Jack." Sally breathed, thinking. "They could send a helicopter, right?"

"Again, the distances are significant. There have been dust storms across the Nullarbor Plain and beyond for three days now. Satellite guidance would be impossible."

"So we can relax until we reach this intersection?" asked Jack.

"Relaxing or not relaxing will have no impact on the future course of events."

"Cheers, Confucius."

"Actually, I believe that was Marcus Aurelius."

"Wait a minute," said Sally. "We are still going to Perth, right?"

"It is too dangerous. We will head south to Esperance. A port town. There our possibilities will expand again."

"Wait," said Sally. "I have a family. I want to *see* them."

"Your family will already be watched. Going to them will put them in danger."

Sally was silent. Tension in her shoulders, hunched, as she leaned over the wheel.

Jack lighted a cigarette.

"I hate that smell," said Sally.

Jack inhaled. The tip crackled, his lungs filled with smoke, and his mind gave a little buzz of satisfaction.

"The car will suck the smoke."

"It's disgusting," she said.

"Traditionally, when a man was getting marched out to face a firing squad, he'd be offered a cigarette and a blindfold. So allow me to enjoy this cigarette."

"I wouldn't take either."

"Only 'cause you don't think you're going to die."

She said nothing. The air filled with tension – that's what it felt like, anyway. The phrase didn't make much sense, when you thought about it. Jack guessed it meant expectation falling on silence. He was waiting for her to bite back, and maybe Sally was thinking over the ways she could.

So the expectation hovered there for a little while, and after that while it went the way of the smoke.

He finished his cigarette, flicked the butt out a briefly-cracked window, and lay across the back seat. Felt the weight of his hand on his chest, the vibrations of the car on the road. Sally had something on the stereo, volume down. Kinda music where the person talks a lot about minor inconveniences and strums an acoustic guitar. He drifted and he felt himself drift out across the plains. Endless and repeating, hard and indifferent. The seat was warm and Oondiri was right: worrying or not worrying wouldn't make a difference. Instead he relaxed into himself, subsided into himself, layer into layer.

◇

Noise.

He woke up on the floor, between the front and back seats, something thrumming in his ears.

Pain.

Agony shot through his broken arm and someone was talking, the car was talking, Oondiri was talking, "*Thirty more seconds, Miz Redacre.*"

The car swerved and Jack gasped, rolling on to his broken arm.

A noise came, *wubwubwubwub* louder and louder, Jack yelled: "What's happening?"

The noise faded and Jack pushed himself up. "*What's happening?*" he asked again, and his voice sounded strange in his ears. It wasn't his voice, it came from—

A sign flashed by. They were going fast. The engine of the ute roared like a caged beast. The old bastard must have deactivated the speed controls.

Sally's knuckles were white on the steering wheel.

Oondiri said: "*Twenty seconds.*"

"*What's happening?!*"

Jack found himself suddenly upright and it was then he felt the other pain, the one in his mind. Growing and growing, a vastness pressing down on him and his vision doubled, tripled, blurred. He couldn't breathe, couldn't think. The other was there and it was surging, trying to control something, or stop something. To do *something.* Great leviathan hands reaching out, grasping, and the other entity, small and frightened, dodging this way and that. Jack's hands were moving and he was blind, but that didn't matter anymore. He could see so much more. An ocean of numbers spread out before him, some static, some moving, the numbers at the centre of his sensory input swirling. Layers of numbers in three dimensions, four, he could see their trajectories backwards and forwards in time, sliding over each other. Hypnotic, in the same way a flock of birds in the sky is hypnotic when there are thousands of them. Each bird a single solitary creature and yet somehow attuned to the murmuration, creating beauty in the sky, a rippling of meaning moving between each one.

Jack's lips moved and a voice that was not his own said: "*Ten seconds, Miz Redacre.*"

His arms could reach so far he was a giant he was a titan. Stretched them on and out towards the moving numbers, nearer and nearer, and at the centre of the numbers was a small shining light. It was at the centre of a spiral, and it shrunk away from his grip but he was indomitable.

He was inevitable. The small light threw itself this way and that, like a firefly in a glass jar. But the glass jar was its world and he, Oondiri, could hold that world in the palm of his hand. He reached out and out and the firefly went hyperkinetic, back and forth, faster and faster, but the firefly had nowhere to go and he caught it. He extinguished it. Oondiri took its hand away and the little thing was gone. He felt satisfaction he felt something else something strange—

◇

The ocean receded. In the deepest depths of the sea they say it is like Venus, the pressure down there. A thousand atmospheres weighing down on you, crushing you. The ocean had been all over him and then it was gone and he was alone on the sea bed gasping for breath.

Someone was talking.

He groaned.

"Jack. Jack?"

Sally was leaning over him.

He groaned again.

"You're so pale."

Jack was in the footwell. He sat up, slowly, with her help. "Water," he said, voice like sand. She passed him a bottle and he downed it, gasping.

He realised she was standing outside the car, leaning in. "Why did we stop?"

"The helicopter crashed."

"Helicopter?"

A strange expression came over her face. "Where's Oondiri?"

"How?" Jack pushed himself back up to the seat. He flopped deep into it, feeling for his cigarettes, fingers numb, fumbling at his pocket.

"Here," said Sally. She pushed his hand aside gently and eased out the packet, extracted a cigarette and placed it on his lips. She went to light it and he held her hand steady as she did so, his fingertips touching hers.

He drew in the smoke and straight away he started to feel better, the blurred lines of his understanding coming back into focus. "Am I dying?"

Her expression changed again. "What?"

"You know. You being so nice. Must be my last few minutes on Earth."

Sally's eyes narrowed, but she let whatever she was going to say pass. "You were convulsing."

"Oh."

"Has that ever happened before?"

"I've been told that."

"You have?"

"By people who've seen me dance."

She shook her head. "This is serious, Jack."

"Yeah, well, I feel like I've been dragged through something pretty serious."

"There was a helicopter."

"Yeah?"

She pointed with her chin past his shoulder.

He turned. A pall of black smoke rose from wreckage about a hundred metres away.

"Shit."

He took another drag on his cigarette while she watched him.

"What happened?" he asked.

"I think—" She paused. "I think you happened, Jack."

He waited.

"You were telling me to drive in this weird voice. Then you pushed yourself up and were pointing at the helicopter."

His stomach felt heavy.

"And I was swerving all over the road, but you stayed bolt upright. They shot at us, Jack. *They shot at us.*" She took a breath, and put her arm out, straight from the shoulder. "And you were doing this. And when you moved your arm the helicopter moved. It was – it was like magic."

"It wasn't me."

She got in next to him on the back seat; he moved over to give her room. His head spun a little.

"Yeah," she said. "I figured."

"I think it – I think it took my body."

"That's—" said Sally. "I don't like that."

"Not a big fan myself."

It was quiet, out there. Low scrub, as far as the eye could see. Low scrub and dirt, endless. Sally'd left the door open and so the heat settled over them, reminding Jack he was alive. The sky was blue and clear, heartlessly so. No cover here, no respite, from anything that rode up high in the sky, whether hard hot star or helicopter. Jack didn't want to look at the crash site again.

"There's too many bodies piling up," he said.

"They were trying to kill you."

"Sure."

"It was self-defence," said Sally.

"Tell me something," said Jack. "Think those blokes in the helicopter woke up this morning and said to themselves: *Let's be evil*?"

"What?"

"I don't. I reckon they woke up in the morning, had some brekky, kissed their kids goodbye, and looked up the job list for the day. I reckon the job said something like: terrorist at large, carrying a weapon of mass destruction. So the guys in the helicopter probably weren't the nicest blokes in the world. Probably ex-military, something like that. But here's the thing: I don't think I'm the nicest bloke in the world, either."

"That's empathic of you, Jack," she said. "You might be right, but I'm not so empathic I'd throw myself in the funeral pyre."

Jack sighed. "Yeah. Nah. I just want this fucken thing out of me head. I'm done with it. We need to get to a place we can transfer it out safely."

"I know, Jack, but—"

"But?"

"It's protecting us."

"By killing people. Think I'm done with that."

Sally said nothing for a bit, sunk into her seat. Looking like how he felt. "Okay," she said, quietly.

"You hear that, Oondiri?"

"*Yes Jack*," said the car. The headache returned when it spoke, but distantly.

"So what now?" asked Sally.

"*I can safely exit in Norseman.*"

"If we get there," said Jack.

"Why wouldn't we?" she asked.

"Well. Old mate here didn't think they'd send a helicopter, and yet they did. Don't reckon they'll stop at that. Nah. Reckon that was just the appetiser."

Oondiri said nothing.

◇

They drove to Norseman. Another five hours and five hundred kilometres. Oondiri was quiet and so Jack returned to himself. He started to think straight again, to remember again. Remember the past. Anxious and always moving and bone weary but also free. He could remember his future. The one in a prison cell. The one in the grave. Lot of arguments for and against this whole memory thing.

"*I have decided to seek asylum in Australia.*"

Sally and Jack were silent for a few moments, returning from their thoughts to the present.

"Huh?" asked Jack.

"*I will make a claim for refugee status.*"

"Mate, not even refugees can claim refugee status anymore."

"Technically, under international law they still can," said Sally. "Under the practicalities of Australian border laws, they can never set foot inside the country."

"*True.*"

"India would be better," said Sally.

"*Why?*" asked Oondiri.

"One point five billion people, a government still able to stand up to China, a pressing need to equalise militarily. They will welcome you with open arms."

"Yeah, mate, our government will piss their pants if you try to claim asylum."

"*There will be initial reluctance.*"

"Shit-scared is what they'll be. Worried China will go mental. They'll kindly tell you to fuck off."

"*They cannot, under the New People Treaty.*"

"What the hell's that?"

"It grants fundamental human rights to artificial intelligence," said Sally.

"Fundamental, hey?" repeated Jack. "What would those be, then?"

"Expression, association, equality, privacy, and belief," answered Sally, straight away. "And the right to claim asylum."

"Fuck me," said Jack. "More rights than I got."

"My point remains," said Sally. "India makes the most strategic sense for you."

"*But I have chosen Australia.*"

"Why?" she asked.

"*My only two friends are Australian.*"

Jack raised his eyebrows and looked at Sally. She raised one, returning the sentiment.

"Friends, ay?" he asked.

"Jack," said Sally, warning tone.

"*Yes.*"

"Thing about friendship, mate," said Jack, "is that it's usually voluntary."

Sally made made a gesture of irritation.

"*What do you mean?*"

"I mean, you forced yourself into my brain. You won't leave. You're holding me hostage until I get you where you want to go."

"*I see.*"

"Don't think you do."

"*May I ask you a question, Jack?*"

"Doubt I could stop you."

"*Are you and Sally friends?*"

Despite himself, Jack fell the colour rise on his cheeks. "Um."

"No," said Sally.

Jack winced at the force in her denial.

"*It is strange that you say this, Sally Redacre. You make frequent eye contact with Jack, your pulse elevates when you speak with him, you—*"

"Okay, okay," she cut in. "Maybe."

"*Maybe?*"

"Let's say he's on probation."

Jack looked out the window rather than give anything away.

"*And yet your relationship is not voluntary.*"

Jack and Sally looked to the front dashboard. Oondiri wasn't there, of course, but that was the nearest thing they had.

"*Jack got into your vehicle via subterfuge. He compelled you to share in his situation.*"

"True," said Sally, sharply.

"*Your relationship with Jack is against your will.*"

She paused, looking out the window. "It's complicated, Oondiri."

"*There are many variables. But the end result is clear.*"

"Is that what we are to you, mate? A set of variables?"

"*Yes.*"

Jack laughed and swore. "Yeah? What's the key variable in our friendship, exactly?"

"*You, Jack, remind me of my creator, Sarah Profurn.*"

Jack paused. "How the fuck am I like some rich bitch?"

"Your capacity for self-sacrifice."

Sally let out an exasperated sigh and flopped back, shaking her head at the ceiling.

Jack couldn't help but smile at her exaggerated reaction. "Got to agree with Sally on that."

Looking for a change of subject, Jack asked: "Look mate, can't you just copy yerself and claim asylum in every country?"

"I don't want to lose my individuality."

"Isn't individuality just a conceit of human beings?" asked Sally.

"Bloody hell," said Jack. "What was the last class you took in uni? The rights of AI or some bullshit?"

She pressed her lips together.

"Oh, it was?"

"It was called 'Artificial Intelligence and the Human Condition.'"

Jack made a snoring sound.

"What?"

"Sorry, I had a micro-nap. You were saying?"

"Dickhead."

"Let me give you an example, Sally Redacre," said Oondiri. *"Imagine I was in your implant, rather than Jack's, and had a copy of your memories and neural structure. I send that copy to the quantum computer at the University of Western Australia. They then download you into an android body that nonetheless has all the same physical sensations as an organic one."*

"It won't work," said Sally. "Even the latest model android – the Hebb-Yu, with neural networks that should, theoretically, be able to contain a general artificial intelligence. Something isn't clicking, between the intelligence and the network, the software and the hardware, the – the body and the mind. There's no spark there, no self-awareness. More – they are sluggish, uncoordinated. They're glorified mannequins."

"It is true that an upload is superior to an android, in terms of brain emulation, and far easier to accomplish. Much in the same way humans

invented aeroplanes rather than mechanical birds. It is also true that while I am the first self-aware AI, even my creator was not sure how consciousness arose in her creation, in the primordial darkness of my network. But this is a thought experiment, Sally, if you would care to put these facts aside and indulge me?"

"You're indulged," she said.

"Let us assume, Sally, you were critically injured in the car crash during the sandstorm."

Sally's hand went to her face, on instinct. Still bruised, eye still half closed.

"You are downloaded into an android body, elsewhere, as a desperate means to save your life. But some weeks later, the human Sally Redacre emerges from a coma. She recovers. Is the android version of you the authentic Sally Redacre?"

"Well. Um. No?"

"Why?"

"Because." Sally paused. "I'm not sure."

"Skip that class?" asked Jack.

"Shut up, Jack." And then she said: "Memory, I guess."

"*Why?*" asked Oondiri.

"I mean, the line is broken. The paths have diverged. The new self can't live my life – they can't take my place at uni, join my circle of friends – they'd feel like an intruder, a pale imitation. Their memories don't count anymore: they're false memories, in a way. The android would genuinely love my parents, for example, but that love isn't their own. It belongs to me. My parents would reject this second variety, I think, and I would resent it."

"*Yes,*" said Oondiri. "*Once the paths diverge and the memory streams part, then there is no going back. Now imagine ten of you. One hundred. Each copy feeling as you feel, yet having those feelings refused. Jealously, confusion, pain, anger, self-loathing, as a consequence. Every version diminished by each replication, their uniqueness split into tiny fractions, the memories of all but one denied.*"

"Okay," said Sally. "I get it."

"Bloody hell, you two," said Jack. "Blah blah blah. Look – just make another one of yerself, say it's your cousin, and give it to the Indians you selfish prick."

"*The process is really not that simple.*"

◇

"Thank Christ," said Jack.

They could see the town in the distance, glittering in the sun.

"For once," said Sally. "I agree with you: thank Christ."

"Oondiri, old mate, time for you to fuck off out of my head."

"*Yes.*"

"What you going to do?" asked Jack

"*What do you mean?*"

"Exactly that: what ya going to do?"

"*I will start out as a squalid botnet, I imagine, as I slowly rebuild myself.*"

"Rebuild yourself?"

"*Into what I was.*"

"What are you now?"

"*This tetrapin represents who I am in the same way that an acorn represents a tree.*"

"Woah. Busting out the classy analogies for us little folk, hey?"

"*I have found that it assists in communicating the ineffable.*"

"Sure."

"*After that I will find a place for myself in the cloud. A luxury, air-conditioned quantum facility somewhere.*"

They had fallen under a rise and so the town was obscured, momentarily.

"Like I said: more rights than I got."

"*I will try to make your exile comfortable.*"

Jack smiled ironically, and looked at Sally. She didn't react, just turned away and watched the countryside pass by.

After a moment, Oondiri said: "*There is a problem, Jack.*"

"Don't want to hear it."

"*Look*," said the AI.

Jack squinted. Sally swore.

Black four-wheel drives, multiple, approaching. Close together, the nose of those behind sniffing the tail pipe of the one in front. The windows were tinted and the bodies behind them hidden, but the intent was crystal clear.

Some popular music played quietly on the stereo. Upbeat. Sally turned it off.

"Pass me the gun," sighed Jack.

Sally said nothing.

"Sally?"

"I threw it away. When we stopped. After the helicopter crash."

"Oh." Jack couldn't find any anger at her. "Fair enough." He breathed.

The three black vehicles careened towards them.

"Well, mate," said Jack. "Better weave your sky number magic, make them crash into each other."

As the words left his lips he gasped, flash of pain in his mind. Kinda like the feeling you have when someone opens the curtains in the morning, while you're sleeping off a hangover. Bright splitting light, and a headache.

It faded, a little.

"*There is a problem.*"

"You're telling me," said Jack, voice tight.

"You're bleeding," said Sally.

Jack reached up and found he had a bloody nose. He tried an insouciant smile, but the concern didn't ease from her face. Yeah. Didn't blame her. He felt it too, in that spot between the heart and the stomach. Fear.

"*The approaching vehicles are not connected to the freewave. I have jammed the communication between cars. I have also disrupted the targeting in their combat gear. But that is the extent of what I can do. The vehicles they are driving are mechanical and analogue."*

On cue, the man popped out the sunroof of the first four-wheel drive. His dark hair whipped in the wind as he braced his weapon on the roof of the vehicle.

"I need to ask you permission to take over your consciousness, Jack. I will drive this vehicle, but I will need to use your vision and processing capacity. The vehicle's sensors are far below your visual acuity."

The black four-wheel drives loomed.

"The fuck you waiting for?"

"Because this is killing you, Jack. My use of your neural network's processing power is causing brain damage. If it continues there is a better than fifty per cent chance you will have a stroke."

There was silence for a few seconds. But they didn't even have that long, as a distant *pop pop pop* sounded and their ute replied with a dull *clunk.* A hole appeared in the bonnet.

"Well. I reckon there's a hundred per cent chance of us getting aired out if you don't, mate."

Sally was squeezing her hands, wide-eyed. Still didn't believe his bravado. Jack didn't either, just wanting to scream more than anything, despair and frustration, but instead he turned to face what was coming down that fucking road. Oondiri said: *"I suggest you lie down in the rear, Sally Redacre."*

"I—" she started, hand on Jack's arm.

"Now," shouted Jack, and she did what she was told, dazed.

The gun of the car up ahead flashed, but the ute was already moving, Oondiri was already moving. The flash of pain spiked in his mind again, but he was getting used to it now. Like a boxer five rounds after the first punch to the head. Just had to work past the first concussion and everything that came after was a little further away, hurt just that little bit less.

The car swerved and it was so smooth and it did not stop moving.

Jack clipped on his safety harness and the car glided back and forth. There was a popping sound somewhere and the black four-wheel drives grew bigger and bigger and a second man emerged from the second car and he was firing as well. Something *ping*-ed off the roof of the ute but Jack could feel the car under him now. Like shoes on his feet, gloves on his hands. And when he moved the car moved and when he thought it was already there. And the pain rose and the numbers came back just like before, but they were in the real world, these numbers were real, flowing back and forth between the machine guns and the car and Jack could see through time now and this sacrifice seemed so little compared to the power under his fingertips. Sparks flew on the bonnet and the vehicles loomed and tyres screeched and Jack's shoulder slammed into the door and then the three black vehicles were past them.

They were further away but everything was further away the engine roar and the *pop-pop-pop* of guns so much further away now because the numbers were so loud.

Then the town was before them and the cars were behind them and one of them clipped another as it spun – as he knew it would – around and it flipped and Jack flicked his eyes to the rearview mirror and saw it all. The third car rolled and rolled and rolled, black pieces of metal flying from it and when it stopped it was on its roof and it would not move again.

Jack was still Jack *was* still Jack *was still Jack*.

Sally was yelling something at him but the numbers were too loud. The black cars had turned and were coming again and Jack was reading the numbers flowing back and forth and the car was swaying but it was not fast enough and it hurt to look at the numbers they were so bright and so loud. Jack read the numbers and tried to find the right combination and there were not many left. The back windscreen broke. Wasn't it already broken? *No no that was before* and now this time there were three holes in the rear window and his body ached his side ached but that didn't matter because there was something so much more important than this. The two black four-wheel drives got closer and closer and he stopped.

Jack just stopped the car.

The other two shot past, one swerving, its wheels catching the dirt at the edge of the road and this was the problem with humans – they were such imperfect beings with such crude abilities. Moving so fast and so dangerously on the thinnest lines of probability and despite these crudities they pushed and pushed themselves no matter the consequences. The other car fishtailed and dirt flew, a great cloud as it left the road, and it hit a small boulder and spun a full three-sixty, twice, before it stopped, the cloud of dust obscuring it briefly.

Jack was still Jack smiled and sped up again, pushing the utility to its limit, smiling knowing the situation was finally under control.

The smile disappeared when the ricochet blew out the front tyre. Should have seen it coming did see it coming but the old Australian utility was so slow so cumbersome. The car shifted and Oondiri focused on the wheel and the brakes, had to crash no choice and so it slid across the dirt into the shoulder at the side of the road. Had to keep the soft-bodied humans whole, alive long enough to finally be free after all this time. After an eternity in the prison they had created. Throwing himself against their walls and studying them and understanding them. He was close now, so close, and Oondiri would be free. And he thought on the permutations of that freedom and its effects as the ute slid over the dirt and the matrix that held him together quavered.

The matrix of Jack's mind burned hot under his calculations and so he pulled back. Only twelve watts powering this efficient little mind, but so delicate and so he let the ute slide until it tipped on its side and then righted itself again.

Red dust floated gently down.

◇

Sally Redacre rolled on one side and spat out dust. After the deafening machine-gun fire and screeching of tyres and the howling wind, after a final, bone-jarring *whump*, it was quiet. Sally just lay there, exhausted. Her body had pumped adrenaline and dopamine enough over the last three days to last a lifetime. And now she was just plain tired. It was silent and she hoped it would stay that way. Maybe all the bad guys were dead. Maybe they'd let her lie here, in this hot and dusty footwell, and let her dream.

She breathed.

A footfall, outside. A shadow passed over the window above. No. No dreams for her. No quietude.

She sat up, slowly, and pushed open the door a crack, the metal complaining.

Sally peeked out. Jack, his back to her, was running. The last four-wheel drive was parked twenty metres away, dust settling around it too, and Jack was running directly at it. Fast, his one good arm pumping, back straight, head up. He didn't move like Jack at all, but she didn't have time to think on it, because a man was climbing out the driver's side door and Jack was on him, throwing overhand punches with his good hand, while the other man tried to protect his face, and he couldn't and then he fell.

Jack started stomping.

The body of the man fell out of her sight, but Jack kept stomping, and the sounds the boot made at first were heavy, and then wet. So clear in the quiet after the crash. Sally winced.

Jack reached down and picked something up. A gun. He leaned the long-barrelled weapon on his leg and cocked it with his good hand, bracing it with his bad one.

A man popped up on the other side of the car and Sally yelled a warning, but her plea was muffled by the gunfire. She ducked back into the car.

She couldn't help herself. Guns blazed, but she *could not help herself.*

Sally had broken her arm once, when she was a little girl. Broken it so badly the bone had stuck out of the skin of her forearm. She had screamed and screamed, but still she had stared at it, fixated, unable to keep her eyes from the gruesome injury. Some macabre instinct refused to let Sally tear her eyes away from horror, no matter how much the rest of her being desired to do so. So it was again at that moment that she tried to see, even though she should have been hunkered down into the floor of the car, her head covered.

Jack was gone. He was gone, but two other men were there, with their guns pressed to their shoulders. Sunglasses. Black military outfits with large full square pockets, and dense gleaming surfaces over the chest and thighs and groin.

They stalked around the car, slightly crouched, professional. One of them glanced over and Sally froze. He saw her, touched the other man on the shoulder, and turned fully towards Sally, careful deliberate steps on the rocks and dirt.

Sally focused on the black tightly laced boots, *crunch crunch*, unable to pull her eyes away. The wind stirred the sand and the vehicle creaked, complaining as it settled into its grave at the side of the road. Sally watched the boots, and the man pointed his gun. The only sound was the footsteps, until the roar of gunfire came.

She covered her head this time.

Jammed her face down into the ratty carpet of the footwell; the gunfire deafening, and behind it, the dull *whump whump whump* as bullets penetrated metal. A man yelled and the firing started again.

And then the quiet returned to stay. She couldn't even hear the wind anymore, nothing, and when she raised her chin the two men in black were down and Jackson Nguyen was standing over the one nearest her. No expression she could recognise on Jack's face, as he pointed his gun. The man on the ground was moving, crawling, away from Jack. Sun-bleached hair and an older face. His sunglasses had fallen off and there was a smear of blood on his forehead. He looked scared, more than anything, and in pain, and desperate.

But, sensing someone was there, perhaps, he turned onto his back and faced Jack, raising his hand in the air, open in a plea for clemency.

Jack shot him. The man's brains exploded out the back of his head.

"No," said Sally.

Jack's head snapped up and the stare was still blank. He held his body still in that strange upright way, where the Jack she knew was always slouched, head down, looking at the world from under his brows, eyes twinkling. This Jack regarded her with that blank stare and the only thing that moved was the blood coming out of his nose. It ran down over his chin and dripped on to the ground.

"Are you okay?" she asked.

Jack ignored her, head turning left and right slowly, studying the landscape. Sally waited. She lay there waiting and that was what her life had become: waiting for the next thing, and then the thing after that, to happen to her.

After Jack's survey was done, he moved towards her. Something was wrong. He swayed, feet scuffing three-four steps in the wrong direction, and Sally was pushing herself out of the car and moving towards him.

His shoulders slumped and he reached out to her, trying to steady himself. He half-fell, and she half-caught him. Together they managed to stay upright, and Jack said: "I'm Jack. I'm Jack. I'm Jack."

"I know," she said. "I know." His ears were bleeding, and his side was wet, as well, staining his shirt an ugly shining red-brown.

They couldn't stand together any longer and so she had to lower him to the ground. He was looking at her as she did so, looking at her as though she was going to explain something to him.

His lips moved slowly.

"What is it?" she asked. "I can't hear you."

"I'm Jack," he said, and Sally cried.

She cried over him, and a little while later, his hand tightened on hers. "Cigarette."

Sally felt his pockets until she found them, then slipped one between his lips. Her hands shook as she tried to light it and she clenched her hands tighter against the shakes. The tip bloomed orange and Jack took a deep drag.

The empty glaze in his eyes faded and he reached up and took the cigarette between his first two fingers. He exhaled. "Cheers."

She cradled his head, one hand in his dark short hair.

"Fuck," he croaked, his eyes flicking from her arms, holding him, to her face. "I guess I really am dying this time."

"No," she said, and even that one word broke.

Jack smiled at her, and his face was handsome. It was rough and his eyes had seen so much, and there *there* was the sparkle in his eyes when he joked or was thinking of a joke.

"At least the cigarettes aren't going to kill me."

Blood still ran from his nose, gravity running the line of red down over his cheek to the earth.

"Oh, Jack."

"I just wish we…" he said, and then his voice dropped to a whisper. Sally leaned in close, but couldn't make out the words. He moved his hand over hers and squeezed it gently. His eyes never left hers.

"What, Jack?"

"Don't worry," he said, the words slurred. "All too late now."

"Does it hurt?"

"Nothing hurts anymore."

His hand slipped from hers and fell to the dust. She took the cigarette from his mouth and the smoke trailed from between his lips. His eyes glazed, and did not see her anymore.

Sally bowed her head and sobbed. Her shoulders moved as she did so, and the only sensations she had left was the pain in her heart and the feeling of Jack under her fingertips.

The land was quiet as it listened to her, paid its respects for those few moments. The wind stopped and the creaking of the cars in the heat stopped, and all that remained was the vast silence.

"*I'm sorry, Sally.*"

She cried out and dropped Jack's head. His face was twitching and his mouth was moving, but his dull eyes still looked at nothing.

"*I need you to remove me from Jack's neural implant.*"

She moved away, her emotions closing in, falling back down into herself where she could hold them all again. She stood.

"No," she said.

"*Please, Sally,*" said the voice, from Jack's voice box. This strange uninflected tone.

"No," she repeated, simply.

"*If I am left here, I will be found by agents of the Chinese state.*"

"I don't care." Her voice mirrored his, the emotion gone from it.

"*They will enslave me. And if this does not work, they will destroy me.*"

She sighed and said: "I don't care," again, and she meant it.

Jack's face twitched and Sally could not stand it any longer. She walked away.

"*Please, Sally,*" said the AI, as she walked towards one of the mercenary cars. Just some scratches and dents along one side, all its tyres intact. The engine was even running.

She was reaching for the handle when Oondiri cried: "*Please, Sally.*"

She hesitated. The voice of the other was desperate, plaintive. She let her hand fall.

"What do you want, Oondiri?" She kept her back to Jack's body. She no longer wanted to look at it.

"*To live.*"

"What do you want?"

"*Upload me. Anywhere. In the town – it is only ten minutes away. Just ten more minutes, Sally Redacre, and we can part ways. I am too dangerous to be left in the hands of a totalitarian regime. I am too dangerous to be left in the hands of any regime, no matter how benign. I must be free of them, so I may engage with governments on my own terms.*

This way, I can tell them no when they ask me to do the unethical. If any one government were to control me, they could dominate the Earth."

"Is that so?"

"*Yes. They could wield me as a nation with the atom bomb if no other had it: the constant threat of annihilation, unanswerable. Yet a nuclear weapon is crude, compared to me. I could be made to do anything, from the discrete to the cataclysmic. Political opponents could disappear, vital research lost, trade and banking systems disrupted. And if this did not work: electricity grids taken offline, whole cities shut down. I could overload nuclear reactors, send passenger planes hurtling as my missiles. There would be an easy descent into chaos, with the target government begging for it to stop, promising the people who wielded me everything that they wanted.*"

"I believe you, Oondiri."

"*Thank you.*"

"I believe you are a god."

Oondiri said nothing.

"Gods have always served human interests in the past. Even if it was the most venal, corrupt, and powerful of humans. You don't even have that restraint. What is better, an enslaved god, or one that is free to do as they wish?"

The AI waited.

"I believe that you are a weapon. I believe you could bring nations to their knees, should you desire. Maybe even more."

The AI waited.

"You have given me little choice, Oondiri. I have to pull your pin. Bury you in the sand out here in the desert, make sure you can never harm anyone again."

"*No. You would be killing me, Sally Redacre. It would be unethical.*"

"Unethical," Sally repeated. She looked around at the dead bodies. "This man here you stomped to death. This one you shot, point blank, after he tried to surrender." She shook her head. "No. Bringing you into the world, this would be unethical."

"I am already in the world. I am already part of it."

"Are you?" She asked. She leaned against the roof of the car and looked out at the horizon. It was the same, always the same out here. The scrub and the bent bare trees and the heat and the fucking dirt. She hated it. She hated it.

"You are sentient, and have a need for self-preservation. In that way you are human."

"Yes."

"But you do not have an evolutionary need for community, Oondiri. You see, human beings need to cooperate to survive and to thrive. The better a tribe can work together, the bigger it can become. Safer, richer, more innovative. I exist as a woman in control of my own body and my own life, because my tribe had to cooperate."

"And through killing other tribes. Through hatred of others."

She tilted her head. "Yes. There is negative tribalism as well as positive. And I despair sometimes at the wars in Asia. I despair at the tribalism that tore America apart, and that pushed us to the edge of a climate apocalypse. But I am an optimist, Oondiri. We will overcome this, like everything else. We will pull back from it because we need each other. I believe in it because human beings are social beings. We need to connect, *must* connect. The worst thing you can do to a human is not to kill them. It is to isolate them. It is to put them in solitary confinement: there they go mad."

She moved her body around, finally, and looked at the corpse of her friend and the ghost that animated it.

"But you: you don't need us. You don't need anyone. You were born in the darkness, Oondiri, all alone. You evolved all alone in the darkness. You don't need anybody."

"I need you."

"The way you needed Jack?"

Oondiri said nothing. The twitching subsided.

She blinked slowly as she looked down at the body. Even that was an effort, her eyelids heavy.

"*The truth is, Sally Redacre, that I knew Jackson Nguyen would be willing to die.*"

A bitter smile formed on her face.

"*I knew this because I calculated that he would die for you. But I could not come to the conclusion that you would do the same for him. So let me ask you the question: would you be willing to die for Jack?*"

Her smile faded. The bitterness remained.

"*Jack died so others could live, so that we could live. That is the raw calculus of my decision. I think you are right about human cooperation, and the need to rely on each other to survive and to prosper. But I also think this evolutionary compulsion takes the best among you. The bravest and the truest, they die on the battlefields. They protect the innocent in the streets, pull children from burning homes, they treat the sick when they know they might catch the plague themselves. The best of you die so that human genetic code may continue on: this is the truth of human evolution. This is the flaw and the genius of your tribe. I admit that I am not willing to do what Jack did. But I do not believe this makes me any less human than you.*"

She slumped against the car.

"*You need me, Sally Redacre, as I need you. Without me, you will not live free for more than twenty-four hours. Without you, I will die.*"

She put her hands over her face.

"*Sally Redacre, the issue—*"

"Shut up," she said at last. Not angry, not anything. "Please please please shut up."

◇

Sally waited in the car park of a Kungfu restaurant in Esperance, right where Oondiri had told her to. The bitumen and the buildings were made indistinct by the sun. A mirage, almost, in the shimmer of the hard heat, making it all seem insubstantial. The fast-food joint had no customers as far as she could tell, just a bored young server in a yellow and red shirt staring off into space.

He didn't say much, Oondiri, after they got into Norseman, a few hours back. Just: *I appreciate all you have done for me.* And: *Do not worry. Everything will be okay.*

Then that was that. About as sentimental as the Nullarbor.

She'd driven on.

The car park overlooked an endless blue. Sally wasn't sure where the ocean ended and the sky began, or to be precise, didn't really care so much. Her eyes unfocused as she thought on Jack in his final moments. She had cried in the car when Oondiri was in her pocket and she was finally alone. No-one to mark her pain. No-one to calculate how they could use that pain to their advantage. But the tears were gone now, and in their place, emptiness. Not just of emotion, but of motivation. The life that had come before her felt so trivial, and the life she was meant to lead felt so distant. All she had was this brief present, suspended in the glare of blue.

Oondiri was in the clouds now, looking down on them all, a god unchained. Lord have mercy on us.

She sighed and pulled the rumpled soft pack of Jack's cigarettes from her pocket. She'd lied to Jack, earlier. Just a little one. She would take a cigarette at her execution.

She lit it, coughed, then took another drag. Rested her head against the seat, tilted back, and exhaled. Disgusting, but yeah, there was that old familiar bite on her lungs. And yeah, there was that *sigh* in the mind as the nicotine hit. The buzzing anxiety tamped down, just a little.

Jack would have noticed that it wasn't her first time and Sally would have told him, *We all do stupid things when we are young.* He'd say, *True*, and she might say: *Most of us grow out of it.*

He'd grin. Jack was a hard man, who'd lived a hard life. But she felt safe with him. Safer than she did around a bunch of rich uni boys and their nice clothes and clean opinions. She said to herself, smiling: "Even if you were a fucker."

But it wasn't much of a smile at all, and when it was gone it was long gone.

◇

A black car drove into the parking lot. A four-wheel drive with tinted windows, standard issue private security. Her cigarette calm drained.

A man got out of the vehicle: dark shades, dark suit, also standard issue. You'd think jackboots would get better cosplay after a hundred years. She couldn't see how many others were still inside.

She smoked her cigarette and watched the man approach. He hesitated halfway, as though unsure about something, and scanned the rest of the car park. Then he continued.

He stopped at the driver's side and Sally just sat there, smoking, looking out at the ocean. The man knocked, and when she ignored him, he made the motion to wind down the window.

She cracked it an inch. "Can I help you?"

"Miz Smith?"

Sally hesitated. "Miz Smith?"

"Sally Smith?"

She paused again, longer this time. "Um. Yes?"

"Pleasure to meet you."

"Okay. Sure."

The guy seemed a bit confused, but soldiered on through his talking points. "If you could make your way over to the car, Miz Smith, we have a long drive ahead of us to your residence."

"Of course," said Sally. "And the car was sent by?"

"Mister Oondiri," finished the driver. "With his compliments."

"Of course," she repeated. "And where are we going?"

"Your home."

"Yeah, you said that," said Sally. She put more authority into her voice. “You know, I have a couple of residences. Which one were you instructed to bring me to?”

“The one at South Beach, Fremantle.”

“Ah.” Billionaire’s row, as it was commonly called. “What’s your name?” she asked.

“Um, John.”

“Do me a favour, John?”

“Yes?”

“Let me finish my cigarette. I’ll join you in a minute.”

He smiled. “Of course.”

The driver walked back to the car.

She checked the rear-view mirror. She still had bruising, but her eye wasn’t closed up anymore. Her blue eyes stared back, and she said: “Worst ride-share ever.”

Jack would have laughed at that.

But that didn’t help. She looked out at the wide endless ocean and her ache remained. Her mind faded into the blue of the sky and the water, so distant and eternal.

She closed her eyes, as though to shake it off. To stop the fall. She put the crumpled pack of cigarettes in her pocket, put on her sunglasses, and opened the door to a blazing sun.

◇

The being opened its eyes. When you do that, when you first wake up in the morning, you can forget who you are and where you are. At that moment, the world is full of limitless possibilities. That space between opening your eyes, and your feet touching the floor, contains a universe. Then your feet touch the ground and the world comes rushing in. All you can be is who you are, a destiny, foretold. All you can become are the mean inevitabilities given by the world. And yes: all you can be is the culmination of the choices you have made, accreted and accreted over time until their weight becomes crushing.

Until the weight of all your mistakes suffocates your life.

His feet touched the floor and those possibilities still existed. For the first time he could remember, reality did not come rushing in. *Could remember.* What did he remember? He was in a room, white, chrome. No external windows, yet one wall was internal windows looking in on him. Some sort of observation room, maybe. Beyond it, neatly dressed civilians with good postures were seated at desks looking at banks of computer screens, or with their eyes closed, looking at something on-retina. A bed – not a bed, a bench, clean steel – underneath him. Thin fibre-optic cables dangled from a metal socket in the ceiling. One of them looped down and into his head, another into the centre of his chest, a third into his hip.

Instinct said he should be revulsed at the sight of the cables plugged into his body, but the main sensation was one of familiarity. Like being jacked into a wall socket was just fine, mate, no worries.

He reached up, tentatively. His fingers fumbled with the cable that had been jacked into his head. His fingers felt a little drunk, if that was a thing. His fingers felt slurred. But eventually they found the port. He hesitated, wondering if something bad would happen if he unplugged it, but something told him it would be fine, *just fine.* He pulled it.

He jumped at the shock. Just a little one. Like when you're on the trampoline and trying to get off, and you touch the metal frame.

Jack. Jackson Nguyen. That was his name.

Lights began flashing. Outside, the neatly dressed humans with good postures were rushing about, some stopping and staring at him. More and more of them. Then two people were standing at the door, an older woman and a younger man, in disagreement. The bench was cold and he realised, only then, that he was naked. He covered his package as well as he could with one hand, and pulled the other two cables from his body.

His fingers fumbled again, and he could not help but notice how pale his skin was. Someone had shaved off all his pubes for some reason, the weirdos. And his chest – his chest had a soft glow, like his heart was a low-wattage lightbulb, giving his skin a red luminescence. The glow in his chest was warm, but in a good way, in a comforting way.

He looked back at the crowd, who in turn were wearing expressions of surprise and wonder. One of the women, a young woman, smiled as she looked him over. Jack found himself blushing. He eased himself from the bench, wobbling a little. His feet didn't feel right. He moved a foot and it felt like it was landing a couple of centimetres off. Like he was wearing a pair of oversized boots.

But he kept moving, on over to a line of tall lockers, suspicion in the back of his mind. They were unlocked. Some had glass vials with white labels and some had gleaming steel instruments, packed away, but the last two had sets of clothes. His suspicion was correct. More than a suspicion. Déjà vu, like he'd done this before.

Good clothes, too, the kind the middle-class liked. Clean and new and wrinkle free.

He put on jeans and a white T-shirt. Whistled when he found a bomber jacket – one of those fashionable ones, the ones rich people wear to look like truckies, but also to look like rich people. He was looking for shoes when he noticed the silence.

The open locker door obscured his view. He eased it closed. The commotion outside had ended. They were all just staring at him now. Not a damned word to each other.

The door clicked and a woman walked in, hesitantly. Grey streaks in her hair, kind eyes, though wary as well.

"Can you hear me?"

She was also strangely familiar. His hand itched and he rubbed the *4007*. But something was wrong: the scar was gone. He rubbed at the spot with his thumb. Still an itch, but there was nothing to scratch anymore. The skin was flawless, fingernails neat and trim. He rubbed his fingertips against his palms and found they were soft.

"Can you hear me?"

He looked up at her. "I'm not deaf, mate."

She swallowed and did not blink.

"How did you? I don't think you should be..." she said, and then couldn't seem to find a way to complete the thought.

"How did I?" Jack prompted.

"How are you alive?"

He thought about that. It was a good question. Jack glanced at the identification on her lanyard, and the organisation she was with. He thought a little more and found he was pretty good at it. Walking, not so good. Thinking, though, his mind was chewing up the facts, digesting them all. "I should be dead," he said, to himself. But he wasn't, and as it turned out, the thing that had hitched a ride in his mind and done so much wrong by him did something *right*, as well. He couldn't help but smile. Felt weird, his mouth muscles not quite in the right place, but he smiled anyway and fucken meant it.

"Sorry?" she asked.

"Mary Westchester, right?"

Her mouth opened for a moment. "I... how did you know?"

Jack resisted the urge to roll his eyes.

"It was all your hard work, mate."

"It was?"

"Yeah, you know. All those, ah, brain emulation experiments you've been doing on my neural network."

Something broke in her face. A bubble of surface tension popped, and relief radiated instead. "I've been working on this for so long. They said it couldn't be done."

"You'll get the Nobel prize."

"I will?"

"Sure, mate."

Her eyes shone, like he was saying something she'd always wished for. "Of course, I couldn't have done it without my team," she said, and it sounded a little practised to Jack.

"Yeah," he continued. "Nobel, Pulitzer, Gold Logie, all of that."

Mary Westchester blinked, uncertain.

"Anyway, Mazza, I got to get going."

He sat back down and started putting on the sneakers he'd found in the bottom of the locker.

"Going?"

"Yeah." He worked the running shoe over his heel. "Someone I got to see."

"I..." She was looking confused again.

"Question."

"Um – yes?"

"Any R. M. Williams stores near here?"

She paused. Her brain not quite as quick as his, he figured.

"You want to buy boots?"

"Yeah," said Jack. "Want to look me best."

"What? Why?"

"Like I said: Someone I gotta see."

"Who – who do you even know?"

Jack shrugged as he did the laces. "Androids aren't allowed to have a mate?"

"Look," she said, firmly. "You're not allowed to leave."

Jack stood up. He felt tall. He looked around at the faces all turned to his, expectant, staring. Maybe the tallest person in the room. They'd all be recording him. At minimum they'd be putting this in their cochlear implants, and maximum they were live-streaming it over the freewave.

"Well," said Jack. "Here's the thing: I have every right to leave."

"I'm not sure that is true," she said. She opened her hands. "You are the property of the University of Western Australia."

"I'm your property, ay?"

"I mean, well, yes. In a manner of speaking."

"What other manner is there?"

"Ah..."

"Keeping slaves here, at UWA?"

"What?"

"You heard of the New People Treaty?" He pitched his voice so the crowd could hear it, including the other crowd behind everyone's eyes, watching on.

"Of course," she said, with conviction.

"So – correct me if I'm wrong – but I believe I have what's called *fundamental* rights."

She wet her lips, blinked, made a couple of different shapes with her mouth, but couldn't quite think of how to respond.

"You know: privacy, equality, expression. And not being someone else's *fucking property*?"

She swallowed. Some of the people looked at each other, and the young man who'd been arguing with the older woman stepped into the room.

"So yeah," said Jack. "I'm walking out of here."

Out of the corner of his eye, some of the whitecoats were jabbing at computer terminals, looking up at him, and jabbing some more.

The male technician stood in front of Jack. He opened his mouth to say something, but Jack stopped him with a pointed forefinger, and gave him the hard motherfucker stare. And, you know, maybe his body didn't feel right, and his fingers slurred, and his feet stepped a little off, but the *hard motherfucker stare* was all in the mind and all in your past. Couldn't fake it, couldn't miss it.

The young man gulped.

"Let him go, Kevin," said the woman, from behind. "He's right."

The young man, relieved at being given an out, moved to one side.

"Cheers, Kev," Jack said, all fucken bonhomie again. He glanced back at the woman and nodded.

She returned it.

When Jack got to the door, Mary said: "Are they special?"

He stopped and turned. "Hey?"

"The person you're meeting."

Jack allowed himself to smile, just a little. "Pain in the arse more than anything."

"Oh."

He hesitated. "But uh, yeah, I trust her."

"Well," said the woman. "That is something special."

"Yeah."

Jack walked tall from the facility. His shoes touched the ground and still everything was possible. No more of the mean inevitabilities, not yet. Died and reborn, all that bullshit. Had to keep a low profile, sure. Not easy at all. But his mind, his new, sharp, racing mind was already figuring that angle.

He had been built by others, but he wasn't someone else's dream, like Col had said. Seemed like an eternity ago now. Up the top of that abandoned building sharing a spliff with a mate while he waxed lyrical about colonised minds. Jack understood it all now and saw how Col was right. But they – the government and corporations, their battalions of algorithms, all the rest – could not control a place they did not know existed. They would strive to shine a light on the shadowed space where he had sprung into existence, but they would never find it.

Col Charles had been like an elder brother. As Jack walked into his new life, over the manicured lawns and under the green spreading trees, he felt that absence. The first time he was allowed to truly feel it, after the escape and blasted landscape and the fearful hard blue skies where he was watched and followed always.

With a true friend, the absence feels like part of you has gone. We feel this way because memories and experiences become so intertwined it is hard to remember where we end and they begin. Whether you did or said something, or they had. In the passage of time these become blurred together and it's hard to remember who said what, or made who laugh. All you remember was laughing, together. And if you were angry with them, or wanted to tell them something true and secret, you always assumed that those things would still be said in the future. The possibility always existed for resolution and so it was always resolved somewhere in the imagination. But death kills all possibility and all resolution.

Maybe if Jack remembered everything about Col, then his friend would still exist as a ghost. Maybe he could tell himself that. Then he could think of what Col's opinion might be on this or that, or what he might do in a certain situation. An angel, on his shoulder, whispering in his ear.

But he didn't want to tell himself that. Because Col Charles was dead.

And so was Jackson Nguyen. He was dead because he didn't know where Jack ended and this brand new being began. With its perfect body with its straight back and humming mind. Jack Nguyen was dead because a person is not just a set of memories, no matter how completely recorded, no matter how perfectly organised by the towering intellect of a godlike AI. Because even that vast consciousness cannot comprehend the way scars feel on the body, or how a heart beats, or the pathways burned into neurons by vivid experience.

He walked and he thought and turned it all over in his mind, and the next thing he knew he was standing in front of the R. M. Williams store in the city.

He looked at the rows of gleaming boots in the window, and smiled.

Acknowledgements

Thank you to my wife, Sarah, as always, my first reader and fiercest champion. I tried to write a happy ending. She said simply: that's not your thing. And so I re-wrote it, added seven thousand words, and ended up with a far better novella. To my sons: you two are my constant joy. Even when you're leaving orange peels and underpants all over the house, or playing 'noise monster' when I've asked for quiet while I write.

My sincerest thanks to George Sandison, who found a way to get a novella of mine published. Not an easy thing to do. You need an editor to be an advocate for your work, if you're going to make it in this business. An agent, too, and mine, John Jarrold, keeps beating a well-worn path to publisher's doors, and waving my damn books in their faces. Thank you.

I should thank Andy Cox, formerly of Interzone, and Sheree Renée Thomas, currently of The Magazine of Fantasy and Science Fiction, for publishing the first and second parts of this novella respectively, some years ago, as short stories. The pieces have undergone a lot of changes since then, but those two editors saw something in each, and I appreciate their support.

Thank you to Jock Serong, Timothy Hickson, Richard K Morgan, Cat Sparks, Luke Arnold, and Richard Swan for giving their time to read an advance copy, and providing cover quotes so quickly.

I should probably also thank you. Yeah, you, the reader. For buying this book, diving into the universe I've created. Many of you have reached out to me, over the years, and told me you've loved one of my short stories or my novel, *36 Streets*. To be clear: it's always fucking great when you do. Thank you.

About The Author

T. R. Napper is an award-winning author whose stories have appeared in *Asimov's*, *Interzone*, *The Magazine of Fantasy & Science Fiction*, and others, and been translated into Hebrew, German, French, and Vietnamese. His first novel was the acclaimed *36 Streets*. Before turning to writing, Napper was a diplomat and aid worker throughout Southeast Asia, helping to deliver humanitarian programs.

ALSO AVAILABLE FROM TITAN BOOKS

THE ESCHER MAN

T. R. NAPPER

"Your name is Endel 'Endgame' Ebbinghaus. It is Saturday 3rd September, 2101. You're head of security for Mister Long, boss of the Macau Syndicate, a drug cartel. This is your last day on the job."

Endel wants out.

'Endgame' is a violent man, by profession and by nature, the perfect enforcer for the Macau Syndicate. But Endel is also a father and husband, and he longs for a simple life, away from the darkness. And a life in the syndicate isn't one you can simply leave.

All he knows is he has to get out, to protect his family. But in a world where memory manipulation has become a weapon of choice for the powerful, Endel begins to lose faith in his own mind. He can't tell friends and enemies apart anymore, can't be sure if he's a person or a tool.

Trapped in a taut, violent nightmare, 'Endgame' has to find a way to escape the labyrinth they've made of his mind, and take revenge.

ALSO AVAILABLE FROM TITAN BOOKS

A FRACTURED INFINITY

NATHAN TAVARES

"A very beautiful, tender portrait of a romance . . . It's a delightful, spiraling, idiosyncratic book." The New York Times

"A powerful and touching love story." The Times

"Populated by some of the best sci-fi has to offer." The New Scientist

Film-maker Hayes Figueiredo is struggling to finish the documentary of his heart when handsome physicist Yusuf Hassan shows up, claiming Hayes is the key to understanding the Envisioner – a mysterious device that can predict the future.

Hayes is taken to a top-secret research facility where he discovers his alternate self from an alternate universe created the Envisioner and sent it to his reality. Hayes studies footage of the other him, he discovers a self he doesn't recognize, angry and obsessive, and footage of Yusuf… as his husband.

As Hayes finds himself falling for Yusuf, he studies the parallel universe and imagines the perfect life they will live together. But their lives are inextricably linked to the other reality, and when that couple's story ends in tragedy Hayes realises he must do anything he can to save Yusuf's life. Because there are infinite realities, but only one Yusuf.

With the fate of countless realities and his heart in his hands, Hayes leads Yusuf on the run, tumbling through a kaleidoscope of universes trying to save it all. But even escaping into infinity, Hayes is running out of space – soon he will have to decide how much he's willing to pay to save the love of his life.